Also by Steven Key Meyers

Novels

That's My Story

Save the Max Man!

A Family Romance

The Wedding on Big Bone Hill

My Mad Russian

Queer's Progress

Springtime in Siena

All That Money

Nonfiction

The Man in the Balloon:
Harvey Joiner's Wondrous 1877

Plays

A Journal of the Plague Year,
and Other Plays and Adaptations

GOOD PEOPLE

A novel

Steven Key Meyers

Good People

SMASH
& GRAB press

*For those who trod the stage of
the original Catch A Rising Star,
and for its ghosts, who are mine also*

IN ONE RESPECT a cavalry charge is very like ordinary life. So long as you are all right, firmly in your saddle, your horse in hand, and well armed, lots of enemies will give you a wide berth.

But as soon as you have lost a stirrup, have a rein cut, have dropped your weapon, are wounded, or your horse is wounded, then is the moment when from all quarters enemies rush upon you.

—Winston Churchill
My Early Life

Good People

1.

SEATED ALONE on the white-leather rear seat of the stretch limo, Rex Black looked out at Manhattan's wild weather through slightly skinned-looking eyes, a small flat triangle beneath each one. An October nor'easter was lashing the city, wind and rain slicing at it from an unaccustomed angle and doing damage as storms from no other point of the compass can do. Trees fell in Central Park, cars floated in underground parking garages, pedestrians sloshed across streets awash with rising tides and loathsome slime began creeping up through basement drains.

In West 46th Street blurry yellow taxis and black cars stood nose to tail, not moving. But somehow the limo slipped in to claim the width of the piano bar Rex was there to raid, Poor Richard's Cabaret.

"Here we are," said Joey, sitting opposite him. *"Showtime."*

But they waited as winds rocked the car and rain thrummed on the roof. Finally the driver ventured out to open the back door. As his umbrella flared in flame-shaped collapse, Rex and Joey tumbled out and ran under the canopy and indoors.

Platinum locks flying behind eager lighted eyes, Joey burst

in first. He moved with vehement angularity, throwing off speed lines like a Haring, never moving with less than total commitment, never not moving.

"*Frank!*" he said to a tall man beside the door. "Never see *you* here."

"Stepped in for one beer," Frank replied morosely. "And, lo, the rains came."

Rex meanwhile entered and stood against the door. He seemed ill-paired with Joey—self-contained, a good haircut, Italian sport coat, slick features that gave nothing away, gleaming as with a coat of gloss, except that his eyes were dry and watchful. At 35 or so he was a few years older than Joey or Frank.

"*Rex,*" said Joey, tugging at Italian wool, "this is *Frank,* the manager's friend."

Marshaling his features, Rex showed strong white teeth as he extended a hand.

"No kidding? Rex Black."

"Rex is my boss," Joey told Frank. "He's good people, you've heard me."

"Sure," Frank said. Usually litanies of complaint, occasionally litanies of adoration, broadcast wherever Joey was downing his margaritas. Rex owned an uptown comedy club called the Gag Reflex. "A pleasure."

Frank led them around a corner to the end of the bar by the cellar steps. Their passage left a wake of hair being smoothed, collars tugged, itches solved—something of the anxiety a shark passing near a school of fish inspires. At the piano Dooley hit a harsh chord and grimaced.

When Dooley started *Baby, It's Cold Outside,* Margo the waitress stepped up to the mic and together they sang it cheerfully and suggestively. They segued to *Stormy Weather* and *I'm Always Chasing Rainbows.*

The storm had only just blown in, so the club wasn't as empty as it might have been, except that it was Friday, when it should have been full. Everybody was making the best of it, and for once the space — a high-tech takeoff on Art Deco, not warm but very chic — seemed cozy. People drank and chatted, flirting across the room as Dooley embroidered show tunes and Justin the bartender served up drinks. Rose-colored gels washed years off every face, made it an assembly of juveniles.

His fans watched Conor, the manager, helping out behind the bar. The bravest leaned across to give his beautiful brow a smooch. He would shy away laughing, then look back in his cool, assessing way from a face drawn in clean Irish design — cheekbones that cast shadows, tight black curls, blue eyes of painful sensitivity.

Meanwhile Joey and Rex put their heads together, whispering as Rex's eyes moved across the room.

Seeing Frank peel the label off his Molson's, Conor asked, his accent pure Queens, "Ready for another, Dolls?"

Joey spoke up: "Hey Conor, who do you have to fuck around here to get a drink?"

Rex flinched.

"Don't look at *me*, I'm a married man," said Conor. With an access of golden light across his face he put pursed lips across the bar. "Where'd *you* come from? In this *weather?*"

"From my boss's stretch limo," said Joey. "Hope you appreciate the sacrifice."

Margo screamed. They saw her twist her tray around and bop a seated man on the head as his hands vanished up her skirt. Conor vaulted the bar. Joey dove into the melee.

Moments later Conor, Joey and three or four regulars moved for the door, carrying the man by kicking, twisting legs and arms that had them staggering into one another. Rex and Frank brought up the rear. The man was saying "fucking faggots, suck my dick, can say no, she wants."

They lofted him outdoors into the rain. The limo driver looked askance.

"Next door," said Conor.

"Hey, lemme *go*, getting *wet!*" the man said with new clarity. "Lemme *go*, cocksuckers!"

They carried him into the mid-block parking lot. A couple passing beneath an umbrella appeared not to notice.

"Drop him."

They dropped him. The man grabbed for Conor's ankle. Conor kicked him in the side.

"*One*," he told him. "Hands off the waitresses, you horrifying asshole." He kicked again. "*Two*: Stay the fuck out of my bar. *Three* — "

The man flinched but Conor didn't kick. Instead he squatted by his head.

"Or are we clear?"

The man sat up and screamed curses. Conor pushed his face at him and screamed louder: "So you're crazy? NOT AS CRAZY AS ME!"

The man launched himself, Conor's knee caught his chin and he rolled back and lay quiet.

"Thanks, guys. We're getting wet."

They were soaked. Indoors Conor rewarded his helpers with a round of drinks and handed out paper towels with a lavish hand. Margo threw her arms around his neck and kissed him while he rubbed her back in brotherly fashion. He looked more upset than she did. Strength protects weakness: old-fashioned but primal.

He seemed easier after a minute. Margo felt for the pen in her ear and went back to work, and Conor gave Frank a Molson's and asked Rex what he wanted to drink.

"Don't believe we were introduced before the brouhaha,"

said Rex, extending his fingers. "Rex Black."

"*Um, um, um,*" said Conor, snatching back his hand. "Heard about *you.*"

"Like the way you dealt with that guy. Who was he, anyway?"

"Who knows?" said Conor. "Some skeevy jerk."

"Unbelievable night, but I see you're doing business."

"*You* doing any?"

"Called from the stretch: Sold out, 160 seats, two shows."

"*Yikes.* We seat 50 and sell out, like, *never.* Hey guys, want to catch the late show?"

"Who is it?" Rex asked.

"Rosetta Stone? The comedian?"

"She's a riot," Joey advised Rex.

"Gag Reflex material?"

"You might not think so," Joey said carefully.

"How about it, Conor? Gag Reflex material?"

"Couldn't say. Never been."

"Never been to the *Gag Reflex?*" asked Rex. "*Amazed.* Here I thought I owned the hottest club in New York."

The early show ending, a waitress anchored the showroom door open and men and women (mostly men) trailed out to claim their coats and jam beneath the hammering awning to watch the unmoving file of cars. Honks from Ninth Avenue advanced by relays past the club to Eighth. Brake lights going dark, the line eased ahead, then red splashed and only the din of horns moved forward. Rex's limo idled quietly.

Before the door closed and smothered horns and rain, someone new slipped inside, and Dooley broke into Hall and Oates' old hit *Man-Eater.*

"Thanks, Dooley," the woman called, "and fuck *you.*"

"Rosetta!" shouted men across the room.

She checked her red slicker and came around the corner,

her face wet and shining. She nodded at Conor, Joey, Frank; when she saw Rex the shine went incandescent. She knew by sight every club owner in town.

"How's it hanging, Joey? Conor, I'll blow you for a drink."

"Keep your lips off me, bitch."

He handed her a Scotch. She sipped daintily, ignoring Rex, who meanwhile showed his teeth again as he asked Frank, "What do *you* do?"

"I proofread at TIME Magazine, Saturday nights."

Rex's smile expired. Rosetta drilled into Frank from the other side.

"There must be more to you," she said. "You're a *writer*, aren't you?"

He admitted it.

"I *thought* so."

She waited. Her dark eyes, limpid and sexy, had an unsettling quality, perhaps owing to her half-Asian ancestry. It was as if the East in them transfixed you while the West knocked you out.

"Working on a play," Frank said. "Adapting Daniel Defoe's book *A Journal of the Plague Year*? I call it *Foe*."

"Great title," Rosetta said dryly. "Love to read it."

"Really?"

"Conor's isn't far from me, I'll come by, if that's OK."

"Rosetta," Joey said, "know my boss, Rex Black?"

She looked affable but blank.

"How nice to meet you. Believe this weather?" She turned from one to the other like a cat rubbing its face, marking its territory. Then she squeezed Joey's ass. "So glad you came for my show. But now I must dress."

Gravely she went downstairs.

Rex asked Joey, "What do we do now?"

Joey hooked a thumb. "*Amscray?*"

But first Rex gingerly approached Conor's ear. Joey leaned in close.

"Conor, know *why* the Gag Reflex is SRO tonight? In the middle of a fucking *hurricane?*"

Conor shook damp curls.

But Joey was bursting: "Because *'Comedy is the rock and roll of the Eighties'!*"

"Fucking *Rolling Stone* said that," Rex snapped. "Got plans up there. Drop by, my guest."

"Thanks," said Conor.

"Seriously, making some changes. Hope Joey hasn't breathed a word — top secret — but someone knows how to run a room like you do, find it worth checking out."

"Conor, you've *got* to," said Joey.

"Hey, I'm there."

Rex had what he came for, so when Dooley announced the late show, causing a flow into the showroom, he and Joey beat it. Rosetta, ready for the stage, passed through the bar, pausing at the showroom door to allow applause to engulf her. Then she went in and the closing door muffled the clapping, made it sound far away, like the rain.

Rex and Joey, cocooned again in the stretch's white leather, headed uptown.

2.

A FEW DAYS LATER, Frank wrapped up his daily stint with a stingy muse. Every day's work saw another few lines excised from *Foe* as he carved his play to leanness. The lesson of its New York Theatre Workshop reading was that it was too long. The danger now was that it would vanish utterly.

When he was finally done for the day, he walked down Ninth Avenue from Hell's Kitchen to Conor's apartment in the Village. Conor lived on Bleecker Street near MacDougal, or rather they both lived there, while Frank used his own tiny place for writing; in New York, true love's no reason to give up a rent-stabilized apartment.

He walked in the wash of a yellow-gray sunset over Jersey. The city was drying out after the storm, and the air was rich with evocative autumn scents of dying things.

Their friends—two distinct groups—thought Conor and Frank an unlikely match, however good they looked together, but Conor was intrigued that Frank found literature more vital than the hectic bar life that absorbed him, while Frank admired Conor's easy authority in that world, his ability to make things happen, whereas his own friends seemed to specialize in formulating anxious putdowns. They'd been lovers three years.

Frank found Conor sprawled beneath a quilt in his La-Z-Boy watching *Sam the Car Man* on public access.

Sam was 16 years old. His show — the only one that could halt Conor's march up the channels, remote aimed accusingly at the screen — consisted of half an hour's tight focus on his cute features as he excitedly answered callers' questions on matters automotive. Half open like a boy's, half guarded like a man's, Sam's face gushed personality through saucer-sized eyes.

As usual Conor muted the sound so talk of fuel injectors or torque converters couldn't distract him from concentrating on Sam an intensity of regard Frank wished he would bend on *him* sometimes. The effort dug fascinating declivities in Conor's face.

Of course, Frank also found Sam mesmerizing. Every time he watched he glimpsed new qualities, as though they were lovers.

"Think he shoved his chair back again?" Conor asked.

Frank studied the screen. From time to time Sam broke off to look aside; there was something touching to his suddenly presenting his nose's acute arc. Until a few weeks previous that movement had put his profile off-screen, whereas now blue framed his whole turned head.

"Maybe," Frank answered. "Conor, hand me the phone. I've got a question for Sam."

"About polishing your dipstick?"

"About where he got those big eyes."

With a charming shy smile Sam made the peace sign and the show ended.

"Eaten?" Frank asked with a caress of Conor's hair.

Conor wore what he slept in — football jersey over gym

shorts — though he'd been up since noon dealing over the phone with sick waitresses and performers wanting to know Brat the booker's *exact words.* He ducked out from under Frank's hand and stood up.

"Yeah," he said. "Or later. Joey called, going up to check out the Gag Reflex with him."

"Is that what the other night was about?"

"Who knows?"

"You hit it off with Joey's boss."

"Seems like a nice guy," said Conor.

Stubbing out his cigarette, he went into the kitchen, started the shower and stripped. He peered into the mirror with his customary expression of surprise, touching one lush eyebrow and leaning closer.

Over time Conor had ingeniously transformed his ground-floor tenement flat into a very gay nest. He built a massive loft bed, complete with stairs, put the La-Z-Boy and a sectional sofa under it, replaced the original kitchen bathtub with a shower stall, and knocked out the wall between living room and kitchen (leaving the doorpost for support). The tiny bedroom he turned into a big closet. Filling every possible space and surface (but very tastefully) was his collection of found objects and *tchotchkes.*

Of course, the place was a cave, its only sunlight a steep slant that derisively gilded the curtains at noon. And the john was in the hall.

"Rosetta called, too," Conor said. "She's coming by."

"About my play?"

"Careful with that one, Dolls," he said, stepping into the shower. "She's *weird.*"

Frank found a copy of *Foe* and started crossing out lines he'd cut since its last Xeroxing.

After a meditative quarter hour being sluiced by hot water,

Conor stepped out, dried himself and began to shave.

Frank put down his script and watched greedily. Conor's nudity was somehow extra-naked, as if along with his clothes armor and weapons also were put aside. Going over and putting his chin on Conor's shoulder, Frank ruffled the hair beneath his navel and scooped up his black-nested cock and balls and tried to engage his gaze in the mirror.

"*Don't*, Dolls, make me cut myself."

"Come, my love —"

"*Do-on't!* Joey's coming."

Both spoke facetiously. Conor's body responded — Frank's hand briefly held more than it grabbed — but he twisted away and finished with a self-absolving cloud of baby powder shaken on so heartily it threatened to blot him out of existence. He walked into the closet — his buttocks two new potatoes pushing past each other — and pulled on his jeans.

Someone buzzed. Frank padded out to the street door and let in Joey and Rosetta. When they came in Conor had donned a retro striped shirt inherited from his father — his parents had both died the year before — and was working gel into his hair.

"Ran into each other," said Joey.

"Hullo, Conor," said Rosetta. "So this is where the man lives, is it?"

Though she couldn't be seen to stare, she took it all in.

"Coming with us?" Joey asked Frank.

"Can't, thanks."

"So what's the story, Joey?" Rosetta asked. "Your boss chasing Conor?"

"No idea," Joey said. Rosetta stared, amused. "I just know he's got big plans."

"As in?"

"As in, I really have no idea."

"Enjoy my show the other night?"

She knew they hadn't been in her audience.
"Sure."
"Rex say anything?"
"Not really."
"Let's get going," said Conor, rescuing him. "*Ta-ta.*"

3.

MIKE OFFERED TEA. They sat down on the sectional.

"Wow, look at the work he's done on this place," Rosetta said. "You and Conor interest me, you know. I mean as a couple. He's working class, isn't he?"

"In this country —"

"That's right, I forgot: The classless society. Tell me, when you watch TV, who holds the remote?"

Frank laughed.

"But that tells me who wears the pants, you see."

"We don't watch much," he lied. He handed her his script. "I'm flattered you want to read this."

"I'm sure it's good. Is it a metaphor for AIDS?"

Frank explained why his adaptation of Defoe's chronicle of London's 1665 bubonic-plague epidemic was not a metaphor of any kind, concluding, "But if it helps people think about AIDS, so be it."

"Frank, why would *you* want to write an AIDS play?"

"For any gay man AIDS is the topic of our time. We're in the grip of something bigger than we are. London under plague? That's New York 1986. But Defoe can relieve a little of the *specialness* of our epidemic, help all this death yield something to us, the living."

"Think Death needs help, do you?" Rosetta asked absently.

She was studying a photo panel on the wall, souvenir of a trip to the Most Enervating Place On Earth. Conor and Frank were never closer than when, after a day at Disney World, they mutually confessed they wanted out, hang their three-day tickets. But at least they had half a dozen souvenir snapshots kindly taken by passing tourists that showed them with Frank's arm around Conor, Conor brightly pointing to a sign next to him that read *Picture Point*.

"Cool," she said. "Are you HIV positive?"

"Hope not."

The HIV test was new and, ensconced in a relationship as he was, Frank felt no need to get it.

"I'd *want* to know," said Rosetta.

"We're faithful."

Seeing that he believed it, she looked him up and down.

"*Mmm*, young American white bread. Know how *succulent* you'd be, roasted?" She smiled toothily.

She billed herself as *Rosetta Stone the Man-Eater* and in her act claimed she was raised by cannibals. She started every set by gnawing at the microphone: "*Gnnnh . . . Gnnnh . . .*" "I'm from the Philippines," she might say. "Mama was a bar girl." (Face lowered, she looked the soul of Asia.) "Daddy was a sailor—Seventh Fleet. Or so they tell me." (Chin up, thrusting out her breasts, she was an Anglo pinup.)

She talked about how the man-eating ways of her mother's people helped her survive in New York (not that cannibalism exists in the Philippines). Hinting at Chinatown sources, she described the taste of different organs, how some are best raw, others better lightly sautéed, and proclaimed the world's tastiest flesh to be that of the young white American male, and wondered whether the reason is his predigested diet of fast food or "possibly the hypocrisy you're steeped in from birth. Is *that* the special marinade? The secret sauce? Feels so good to skin one of you motherfuckers, chop you up, throw you in the pot, eat the whole mess and next day flush it down the toilet. Feels so *right*."

The laughs always stopped, though it was surprising how long keeping a smile on her face and a complicit light in her eyes could jolly an audience along. But the moment came when people, if nominally still snickering, began to turn their backs to the stage and commence waiting her out. Rosetta, with ten years in the stand-up comedy game, had no idea why the break she was desperate for was so long in coming.

"Tell me," Frank asked, "how much of your act is true?"

"Artistically speaking, it's *all* true."

"You've *eaten — ?*"

"I say so, right?" she said. "Go on about it, even. But *you* try coming here, no father who wants to know you, not speaking the language except pidgin, after growing up in a *hut* with a *hole* in back, with people who hate you *because* your dad's American, and end up at Columbia, where no one will even *talk* to you —"

"OK, OK," Frank said. "I *see*."

"I know you do," Rosetta said equably. "I could stand up like everybody else, talk about how awful my last date was or what a shit the President is, but I think performers — *all* artists — have a responsibility to tell the *truth*.

"You owe it to your own integrity to give people the truth, but also it's what they *need*. They may not know it until they hear it, or even then, but that's what comedians are *for*, Frank — to get the audience to see what it looks at every day in a more honest light.

"Truth hurts," she said. "I'm the first to say it. But comedy *comes* from pain. We laugh at what hurts. Laughing's the same as crying. Fucked up, but it's human."

Frank tried to look at his play through her lens of truth.

"That's why the same words from someone HIV *positive* — condemned to die young — would have weight *your* words could *never* have, Frank.

"At the Dick," she went on, referring to Poor Richard's by its nickname, "I look at my audience and think how half of them will be dead of Rock Hudson's Disease in a few years (that's what we should call it: Give it a celebrity's name, it's not half so disgusting). And the better half, too. Let them go out with some dignity, I say — *truth* ringing in their ears. Not this Seinfeld shit. Wacky dates."

"He's funny," Frank noted. Jerry Seinfeld had recently broken out of the pack of new comedians and begun appearing regularly on *The Tonight Show with Johnny Carson.*

"So they tell me," Rosetta said, picking up his script and standing up. "On that note. I'll have to be honest with you when I've read it, OK?"

"Of course. Nothing less will do."

At the door she turned around and saw — hanging over the restaurant booth Conor one day dragged all the way home from a Broadway dumpster — a poster enlarged from a photo published in *Blueboy*: Conor, a beautiful love-struck boy in a tuxedo, waltzing a blow-up sex doll wearing a pink Halston through the Greenwich Village Halloween parade.

"Oh, that's *great*," she said. "That's just *too* cool."

4.

CONOR AND JOEY flagged a cab out front. It crossed to Broadway, turned, merged at 14th Street into Park Avenue South, later worked over to First Avenue.

"Maybe I should fill you in," Joey said. "Rex took full ownership of the Gag Reflex last month?"

"Yeah?"

"See, before that he was partners with my old boss Harry Germano? Germano started the club, and that's where he discovered Tintinella. She used to sing between comedians. After she got a record deal and her records started selling, he brought Rex in to squeeze the label—renegotiate the contract. She was the No. 3 seller in North America last year, but Rex and Germano weren't getting along, so they split up: Germano kept Tintinella, and Rex took the club and the other personal-management clients."

"Who are—?"

Joey laughed gloomily.

"No one you ever heard of," he said. "*Yet.* But hey, great acts."

At the 59th Street Bridge they sat through a change of

lights. Headlights streamed off the iron overhead like rhinestones sliding off a bracelet.

"So you went with Rex?"

"Rex is *great*, Conor: Energy, ideas. Yeah, I'm with him all the way.

"Tonight we'll just hang out. Freaks them out when I come in, staff thinks I'm spying. Keep your eyes open and talk about anything but the club."

"Yessir."

"Tuesday's dismal. Hard to get people in during the week. Funny business, running a comedy club. Nickel-and-dime, like any bar."

Joey was another bar person, having tended bar at Jaye's in the Seventies. He still thrilled his friends with tales of each individual Beatle coming in and trashing the others.

At 76th Street the cab pulled up in front of the Gag Reflex. While Joey paid the fare Conor got out and faced the antic neon sign in the window. A tongue unrolled through poufy lips, a knuckle poked through them and letters flashed:

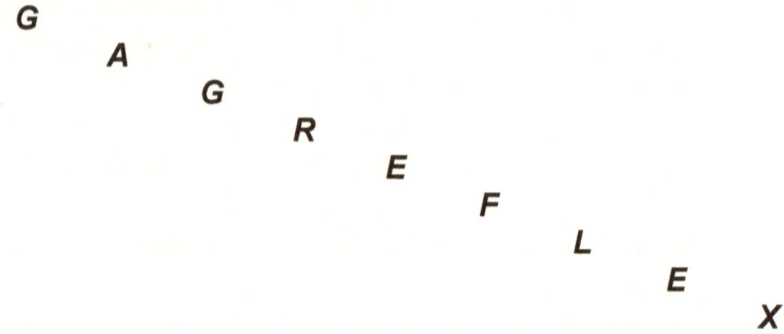

Everything blazed spasmodically, went dark, and started over.

"*Sheesh*," said Conor. "That's *gross*."

"Classy, compared to before: Place was a strip joint?"

"Maybe add neon puke? Just an idea."

Joey led him inside. Conor's impression was of smoke, stink, disrepair and demoralization. Shabby carpeting covered the floor. The clumsy bar was of two heights, with a back bar joined of mismatched mirrors. The hanging lights had plastic shades.

"Meet Sly," said Joey. "My friend Conor."

The bartender nodded. He was already grinding ice for Joey's margarita. "What'll it be?"

"How about — Kahlúa?"

"Really? Coming right up."

Conor's tactic — it amused Frank — was to drink what he didn't like, lest he drink too much.

"This is The Wall," called Joey from a stretch of nicotine-stained 8x10 photographs, some signed (to Germano) by the famous, the rest inscribed even more fulsomely by comedians whose eyes held the haunting knowledge of their own oblivion. "Our famous Wall."

"Shit," said Conor.

"Catch the show?"

"Whatever."

They carried their drinks through leather curtains into the showroom. It smelled. To one side was a low platform. Above it lights illuminated the club's logo carved in wood, more clearly a rip-off of the Rolling Stones trademark, against a plaster wall soiled with flop sweat. A man holding a mic eagerly caught at their entrance.

"Here they are now!" he said, and brayed with laughter.

Eight or ten demonstratively silent couples were scattered around the room. Gripping Conor's shoulder, Joey steered him to a table.

"But as I was saying," the comedian went on, "I've dated more than my share of dogs."

After a few minutes of this Conor started laughing at its

sheer desperation. Naturally his laugh triggered Joey's infectious giggle. Others took it up with an ironic wheeze.

"What'd I say?" beamed the comedian. "What'd I *say?*"

A few sets later a woman whose tilted head fenced off her face with hair came up to their table.

"Are you Conor?"

"Hey, Coral!" said Joey. "Meet Conor Brennan. Coral's general manager."

"Charmed," said Conor.

"Rex Black is on the phone for you," she told him.

They looked surprised. Coral took them downstairs through the Dutch door at the end of The Wall.

"Watch your head," she cautioned.

Conor had a fleeting view of a junk-filled cellar before Coral installed him at a wobbly desk in the office. It was a tiny afterthought of a room wedged beneath the staircase, its five-foot ceiling covered in carpeting, with walls mirrored for that claustrophobic effect beloved of New York interior designers. In leaving she closed the door. Conor pushed it back open and punched the blinking button on the phone.

"This is Conor."

"*Conor!* So how you like my shithole?"

"Quite a place, Rex."

He saw Coral leading Joey past three-legged chairs, an upended desk, cardboard cartons blooming with moisture and through a door. A light went on and he saw liquor bottles shelved against rock walls. The door closed.

"Look to you like it could make somebody *thirty million bucks?*" Conor was silent. "Serious, that's what Tintinella's done—*net*. No wonder Germano's out of there, who needs a smelly hole on First Avenue when the money's coming in too fast to count? Poor me, that toilet's all I *got*. Meet Coral?"

"Yeah. Nice lady."

"Oh good, so she's not doing her coke right in front of your face?" Rex asked. "Germano put up with it, wouldn't even care to guess why, doesn't bother *him* that John Belushi used to score drugs there, or that it says so in a book 17 weeks on the New York *Times* bestseller list, but *me?* A, I hate that shit, B, I'm turning that place around. Joey tell you?"

"About—?"

"My plans?"

"Not a word, Rex."

Conor saw the door in back open and Coral and Joey hilariously emerge. Coral went upstairs. Fussing with his nose, Joey came into the office and bumped his head.

"Big man still on?"

Conor covered the mouthpiece.

"Go away, Joey, we're reviewing your salary."

"Knew it! He hired you?"

"Nah. But he's talking. And talking."

Joey withdrew and Conor pulled the door to. It was like sitting in a packing case. He undid a shirt button. Rex was saying, "—fill you in soon, has to be need-to-know for now, but look around, you'll see what I'm up against.

"Breaks my fucking heart. Sit down with Mr. Clive, poke my fingers up his yappy little dog's ass, hold it out the window and get three cents more on the dollar *and* songwriting credit? *That* I can do. Make clients Germano couldn't do *squat* with into *stars?* Piece of *cake!* But the fucking *bar* business? Wouldn't know how to get *started*, and with the jerk-offs I got working for me—"

A buzzer sounded and another light on the phone flashed.

"Rex, hold on a sec?" Conor tapped the *Hold* button and the flashing one, and heard a clamor of voices and a cry, "Coral's passed out!"

"Be right there," he said, and ran up the steps. Joey met

him at the Dutch door.

"S'OK, man, she's fine."

"Where is she?" But he could see her, swaying atop a stool, laughing, red-faced, as Sly held her face in his hands and spoke into it. "She was out?"

"Conor, she's *fine*. We'll put her in a cab."

He went downstairs and found Rex's line dead. Another line flashed. The buzzer sounded.

Punching a button, he said, "*Yo?*"

"Rex Black on line two."

He hit *Two*.

"Conor, never, *never* put me on hold."

"Little crisis here, Rex, your manager passed out."

"*Shit!* What I fucking tell you?"

Line one lighted up again, and the buzzer sounded, but Conor ignored it. Rex was going on when someone banged on the door. Joey came in and said tersely, "Conor: Joe D. on one."

"Rex, I know I can't ever, *ever* put you on hold," Conor told Rex, "but some shmo named Joe D.'s on line one, and —"

"*Shit! Take* it, for fuck's sake!"

Conor pushed buttons.

"Yeah, this is Conor?"

"Conor, Joe D. Would you please ask Miss Coral to remind Rex Black that the month ends next week, and he never got back to me *last* month, and this just *cannot* go on?" The voice, grainy and gaspy like Darth Vader's, seemed to take pleasure in its own low tunefulness.

"Yessir, I'll tell him."

"Thank you, Conor."

Back to Rex.

"Joe D. reminds you about the end of the month?"

"*Fucking SHIT!* Didn't say I was on the line, did you?"

"No."

"Look, Conor− (Go back to sleep, Perri, it's nothing) (Look what that goombah did, woke up my wife! Fucking *gorilla!*)

"What it is, I'm making changes up there, I really am, but I have to take it slow. Right now, City's threatening to shut me down: Code violations up the *wazoo*. No choice, have to clear 'em before anything else. Need a point man on it. Joey says you do carpentry, all that shit. Be a way of getting in, seeing what's what without anyone feeling threatened or hiding stuff. And then, you want, we talk.

"Don't know where you're going with your *piano* bar, what kind of fucking career path *that* is. Working your way up to running a *gay* bar? *Hmmm?* 'Cause what's coming down for the Gag Reflex is ten times−ten *thousand* times−more exciting!"

"Uh−"

"Don't give me that, Conor! How long you see yourself opening beer bottles in a freak show? *C'mon*, think of the future."

"What code violations?"

"City wants− What *don't* they want? Junk cleared out of the cellar, that carpeting upstairs *out*, sprinklers working. Endless! It's that fucking Coral, no idea how to do business in New York: You meet the inspector, find out what *his* problems are, do what you can, everything's copacetic. And cheaper, in the long run. I mean, that dildo you work at? Bet it doesn't have any violations hanging off it−over there you know the last word on *grease*, am I wrong?

"Come by the office, that's all I ask. Will you at least the fuck do that?"

"Sure, Rex."

They hung up.

5.

REX HAD CALLED from home, sitting in his briefs in the alcove study of his apartment in Ruppert Towers, off York at 91st Street, where he and Perri had lived since their marriage four years earlier. Down the hall sheets were restlessly shifting.

He went into the bedroom.

"Wake you?" he asked softly.

"Yes," said Perri. "No, I was awake."

Sitting down on the bed, he put a hand on her hip and gave it a rub.

"Sorry, babe. That guy Conor's looking the club over right now."

"Good," she said. After a few moments she turned towards him, Rex leaned over, kissed her and, both hands working, eased onto and into the bed, and into her.

Theoretically Perri wished Rex were a gentler lovemaker, someone who would help light her candles, after choosing the scent with care, and give some thought to the music; someone who would then commence a dreamy, unstressed, ever more personal concentration on *her*. Maybe someday, when realizing some of his ambitions had unsprung his general urgency, he would become that lover.

Until then what he offered was all right, because it was so *him*: The incessant pounding, that hammering at the doors that continued after they were thrown open, to explode and finish and go away until next time; this hardness and projection of hardness that unfocussed his eyes, strained his face crimson, made veins pop out like cables threatening to snap, his body one clenched reflex hinged to concentrate its force at a point — this was so *Black*, so *Rex*, finally so *intimate*: He was giving her what he had to give.

They met after Rex graduated from college and before he popped up in the music business — a period he tended to suppress.

College he was perfectly open about. Rex attended SUNY Albany during the bloody later years of the Vietnam War, which he weathered by winning a high number in the draft lottery. He marched against the war, but peace wasn't really his style. This he learned when he volunteered to help organize student concerts. He found that it involved gruesome carnage — double dealing, *triple* dealing with the bands, facilities people, sponsors. It was fun!

His concerts were huge successes — great shows, big crowds, lots of money, none of which adhered to himself (who cares about *money*? Any jerk can make *money!*). Instead he reaped a wealth of contacts. Crosby, Stills, Nash and Young liked him; Joni Mitchell adored him; Jefferson Airplane, Leon Russell, The Band, The Electric Light Orchestra swore by him, and in this life Rex never expected to surpass the day he brought Paul McCartney and Wings to Albany, New York.

But he didn't go into the music business. Conflicted but dutiful, as he'd been groomed to do since birth he joined his father's business and dropped from sight.

He gave it his best shot. Black Restaurant Supply was a profitable concern, useful to kitchens throughout the five boroughs, but it was deadly, at least to Rex. To be hounded by your dad about Hobart mixers? Unendurable.

His solution was to build up the novelty-gift sideline. He put out a line of troll keychains, but so did every Tom, Dick and Harry. Then he conceived his genius idea, a line of coffee mugs customized for every city in the nation: *I Got Mugged in New York, I Got Mugged in Portland.*

His father heard him out, appalled.

"Get it?" Rex asked eagerly.

"Rexaroni," replied his dad, "I wouldn't care to be *associated* with an idea like that."

Naturally Rex quit. Starting a company to make his mugs, he pitched them to the trade at shows coast to coast. That's how he met Perri. Her first job out of college was doing PR for a dinnerware marketer. She set up booths at many of the same shows.

But Rex's mugs failed. Wholesalers would lift them, read them, drop them like hot coals.

Meanwhile his father came out with a coffee-mug line of his own, each mug painted with a frieze of pussycats and the legend "C.a.t. spells *LOVE.*" These made a hit nationwide.

His dad dropped dead of a heart attack soon after, leaving Rex's mother a well-fixed widow. Rex refused her plea to carry on the family firm. Instead, as his own venture gave up the ghost, he began hanging around clubs and recording studios and looking up old music contacts. Soon he was helping a former roadie named Harry Germano extract higher royalties from her label for his client Tintinella.

Rex discovered — *rediscovered* — that what this world attends to is *id. Wanting* something earns respect and attention as nothing else can. Henceforth he manifested himself as pure appetite, and brooked no brakes, no reins, no limits, no possibility of appeasement. "Limits are a *disease*," he liked to say. "Limits say *'Someone please stop me.'*" Like a young Donald Trump, he enlisted everybody around him in the (impossible) effort to satisfy his drives. *Id* gave Rex the energy to fight through everything thrown at him.

"How was it for you, babe?" he asked, as always.

As always, Perri answered, "Great."

She meant it, too. He was a little boy, a naughty, bullying, unashamed, darling little boy going for what he wanted in his monomaniacal, even magical way. Hers to absorb what she could. She watched him curl up into a ball and fall asleep, dead to the world until daylight alarmed him with the consciousness that there was lots to do to get what he wanted.

6.

A FEW AFTERNOONS later Conor found the sooty brown-brick building opposite Carnegie Hall that housed the corporate offices of Gag Reflex, Inc.

The little elevator moaned as, against its nature, it lurched upwards. It disguised its incapacity with a postmodern cladding of stainless-steel plates bolted one over another that gave him back his image aggressively distorted. On the 7th floor he found a door of chipped beige paint with a photocopy of the Gag Reflex logo Scotch-taped to it, and knocked.

"S'open!" he heard.

Going in, he found a residentially-scaled room (the building originally apartments), carpeted, furnished with three desks and a sofa, lighted by standing lamps and windows facing an airshaft. Gold records lavished the walls like seals of approval.

The receptionist, a comely young man bowing his blond head over a telephone, was trying to continue a personal conversation under adverse conditions; his eyes invited Conor to wait. A beautiful woman with long dark hair—Perri—sat motionless in the corner, one hand on a pile of file folders, the other atop a bookcase, listening to a low jangle of something New Age. A scented candle burned in front of her. One wall had a closed sliding-glass door that gave onto a bright office against whose backdrop of Carnegie Hall's upper stories Rex Black paced as if chained to his desk by the telephone cord.

"*Conor!*"

Flying aslant through a doorway, Joey hugged him and introduced him to Perri and to Byrne the receptionist. Rex hung up, came out, showily stripped off his Armani jacket in deference to Conor's retro sportshirt, and showed him around the bullpen, off it Joey's cubbyhole, the conference room and a good 1930s bathroom, tub filled with file cabinets.

"Nice layout," Conor said, settling into a cane-seat Breuer chair in Rex's own, provisional-looking office. The desk was a fine old table, and Rex's high-backed chair was of good leather, although its stiff swivel and rocking mechanisms tended to push him around, but the other furnishings were cheap and the walls empty.

"OK for now, but we'll need more space soon," Rex said. "Possibility we'll knock through, take the floor, but might be better off moving. Neighborhood's good, but between you and I, building's not keeping up.

"Look, I enjoyed our chat the other night. We're able to communicate, and frankly that's not a feeling I get with everyone. I'm being honest."

"Thanks, Rex."

"Know much about my business?"

"Not really."

"OK, once upon a time this dog walks into the Gag Reflex and opens her mouth, and soon as Germano pulls his dick out, lo and behold, can she fucking *sing*: *Tintinella*. Thirty, forty million dollars ago. *Net*. I kid you not.

"Germano brought me aboard to stare down her record

company, I got a piece of what I got them, upshot, we were partners. More or less. He finally wakes up, sees his club's a shithole, wants *her* all to himself, so asks for—and gets—the Big D. Fine, unloads the shithole on *me*.

"But I've got a nose for the zeitgeist like you wouldn't believe. Great word, zeitgeist—and comedy is *it*. '*Rock and roll of the Eighties*'? Fucking fortune to be made from that very shithole!

"And my personal-management clients? Racquel—powerhouse singer, *great* tush, Tintinella feels very threatened—and *should*—and The Come-Ons, Joey swears it's the next big band. Plus one comedian so far, Hank Washburn, totally mainstream, positioning him to replace Johnny Carson, Carson ever retires.

"And my staff is tops! Joey's A&R, he's super, knows *everyone*, Rolodex out to here. And Ashley—you haven't met her yet?—she books the club, she's *super* super. Head on her shoulders? Her great-grandfather was a partner of J.P. Morgan's! And Perri—what can I say? *Invaluable*."

Rex paused, smitten by his own words.

"Hope that club's a producer," Conor remarked. "That's a lot to support."

"*Exactly!* But that's where *vision* comes in. My club? Conor, it's a fucking *hole*, I know that, but comedians come in every night, and so does an audience. Talking stars: David Brenner! Rita Rudner! Hell, Belzer almost *lives* there! Run it right, we'll pack it nightly! They'll pay to get in, pay to drink, pay for T-shirts and—top secret—pay to *eat*. (Yeah, putting in a menu, Perri's tasting right now.)"

"That's great, Rex." Sucking on a cigarette, Conor watched a frenetic dance class over Carnegie Hall.

"OK, OK, time to get naked with you." Conor's eyes veered round to Rex's. "Keep a secret? What we've got in that shithole is a concept, a template, a fucking *franchise*. Only we're too smart to franchise it: We're going to open new Gag Reflexes across the fucking country, but own 'em, book 'em, manage 'em from right here." His voice dropped. "And here's the beauty part. The performers we book? We'll *sign* the cream of the crop — build our roster from the hottest new acts in comedy and music, then move 'em into records, TV, movies, you name it."

Rex leaned over his desk.

"Five years from now? *Hundred million dollars annual net.*" He bit off each word. "Read the business plan, lays it out. 'Cause everyone's looking for the rock and roll of the Eighties? I already fucking *own* it."

The telephone on the credenza behind him — his private line — rang.

"The fuck?" He swiveled stiffly and answered it. "*Hello?* . . . Hey, Joe! Yeah, he did, thanks for the reminder." Rex sprang to his feet and began pacing. "Level with you, Joe? Fall and winter aren't comedy seasons, comedy's more *warm* weather, so the numbers . . . Yeah . . . Yeah? In the mail! . . . You, too, Joe."

He hung up, quivering, suppressed an exclamation and sat down. His chair jerked him backwards, and during its transit his apprehensive Joe D. expression was replaced by his usual expectant confidence. Conor thought he resembled the young George Segal. They shared the same tooth-grinding smile.

Picking a fleck of tobacco from between his teeth, Conor held Rex's eyes.

"TV? Records? National chain?"

"Fucking *A!* I'm an asshole: Forgot the IPO! Top secret, Conor — but I know I can trust you." He leaned forward on bent-back fingers. "IPO means Initial Public Offering. Taking this baby *public* — selling stock, raising *millions. That's* where we get the money to build the new clubs, develop the new stars. Convert our heat into cash, buy *more* heat. Fucking *synergy*—ever hear of it? Stock options are going to flow like water around here. Conor, I'm going to make you *rich*."

At this moment Rosetta Stone, having counted off four, five, six days and glued a résumé to the back of her new headshot, walked boldly into the bullpen. She took it all in as she turned to close the door. She also noticed Rex leaning earnestly over his desk, but could see only the knees of whoever sat across from him. For an instant Rex's eyes darted over and brushed hers.

Joey sprang out of his cubbyhole.

"Rosetta!"

"'"*Joey*,"'" she said, her intonation bracketing his name in quotes within quotes. It was her way. One could infer multiple layers of irony, or of contempt, or in fact whatever one wished ("I imply nothing," she liked to say).

Hugging her, Joey turned.

"Perri, this is Rosetta Stone, we ran into her at Poor Richard's, she headlines there, she's a *riot*." To Rosetta he said, "Perri's Rex's wife."

"Nice to meet you," said Perri.

"Delighted to meet *you*," Rosetta said sincerely.

"And that's Byrne."

Byrne, engrossed, waved from his telephone.

"Are these Tintinella's?" Rosetta asked, looking at the gold records.

"Yes, they are," said Perri. "All we have room for."

Rosetta peered at one. Within the frame and matting was what appeared to be a gilded LP and, beneath it, a brass plate engraved:

Awarded to Tintinella by the R.I.A.A.
Signifying 500,000 Sales of *Love Sucks*.

"Cool," she pronounced. "Lay it on a turntable, do you hear the music?"

Joey and Perri laughed.

"Come see my office," Joey said, but not before Rosetta took a wider-angled view of Rex's and saw Conor smoking with legs crossed.

"Is that *Conor?*" she asked. "What's *he* doing here? Rex buying out Roland?" ("If I want to know something, I ask," she said when anyone asked why she was so direct. "Why not, if I want to *know?*")

"Who's Roland?" asked Perri.

"Owns the Dick?" Rosetta told her. "Rumor is he wants to sell."

"I think it's just a routine meeting," Perri said, opening a folder. Rosetta allowed Joey to pull her away and put her in a chair.

Joey's cubbyhole occupied what originally was a kitchen. It had a desk, two chairs, one square yard of empty floor and, rising to the ceiling on every side, racks and banks of turntables, CD players, tape decks, amplifiers and speakers.

"Cool," said Rosetta. She leaned out of her leather jacket in her favorite *America Beats All* T-shirt. "I'm really grateful to you and Rex for coming out in the storm the other night, wanted to leave my résumé."

"Thanks," said Joey, turning it around and admiring the photo. It showed her smiling maniacally in novelty glasses. "Hey, great picture. Kooky look."

"Joey" — she spoke low — "get me into the Gag Reflex. Onto that stage. People laugh at my stuff. Give them the chance to hear it, they *laugh.*"

"Um, it's not something I do, booking that room: That's Ashley's."

"Ashley hates my guts. The one time we met, had a real

run-in."

"That's OK," Joey said. "Get past it, though, 'cause Ashley books that room."

"She'll take a suggestion from you. She's never seen me perform."

"I'll tell her, no problem."

"And Rex, now that he's seen me?"

"Sure, but we all have autonomy over here, that room is strictly Ashley's. Hey, want to hear Racquel's new demo?"

"'"Racquel?"'"

"Our new girl singer? The new improved Tintinella?"

Handing her a headset and donning another, he pushed buttons and leaned back, his hand thumping the beat while he watched her. She looked back, never blinking until the song ended. She didn't much care for it.

"That's great," she said, taking off the headphones. "Nice to hear fresh talent."

Joey was relieved.

"Isn't she a *knock-out*? And on stage *fantastic*. My discovery."

"Where'd you find her?"

"Been knocking around town for years, getting better and better. Her time has come!"

"You'll make millions off her," Rosetta said.

"Yeah, I think you're right."

"Seriously, what's Conor doing here?"

Seeing Conor in Rex's office seemed to confirm the rumor that Poor Richard's was for sale, and the very idea made her sick. It was the only club that booked her as a headliner.

"Hey, I wouldn't know."

"Fucking Richie had to go and die."

Richie was Roland's lover, co-owner and guiding spirit of their two clubs. But big, hearty Richie had spent a year wasting away to something bundled into a diminutive coffin six months earlier.

"Do you really see Rex going into cabaret?" asked Joey, folding his arms behind his head and looking sage.

"Shit's *raiding* Roland? But Conor *lives* for the Dick: Why would he leave it for some shitty straight comedy club?"

"That's the question," said Joey. "If he comes at all it'll be kicking and screaming."

This was exciting: Her buddy Conor running the hottest comedy room in town? Could set up her big break! Deciding to await developments, she lighted a cigarette. Joey shoved a saucer at her.

"Catch *Letterman* last night?" she asked.

"No, how was it?"

"He did a cannibal joke. Stole one of mine, practically."

Joey shook his head, concerned.

"Don't let him do that. You should go on, stake out that territory for yourself."

"Know anyone over there?"

"Yeah—through Ashley, I mean. She knows one or two people. Not that it helps, can't get Hank booked to save her life."

"Does she fuck them?"

"No, it's all women over there—" He frowned, then laughed.

"Old ways work best."

"I'll remind her."

She smoked. Joey sprawled, legs apart, elbows winging his face. Rosetta, who had better hearing than many in the music business, heard the scrape of a sliding-glass door and a hoarse whisper: "Perri, who's that with Joey?"

"Rosie something?"

"*Fuck!* Get rid of her!" The door slid shut.

"Joey?" Perri called.

Joey jackknifed out of the room and Rosetta heard whispering. Putting out her cigarette, she went into the bullpen.

"Joey, got to run, just wanted to leave my glossy for you and Rex. Perri, great meeting you. Please come see my show at the Dick tomorrow, as my guest."

"Thank you, Rosie, I'll do my best."

Joey stood aside, arrested in a dynamic pose, set to rocket out at any angle. Rosetta caught Rex's eye and spoke up through the glass.

"Rex, thanks for catching my show, Joey says you loved it."

"Absolutely," Rex mouthed, giving Joey a haunted look.

"Just telling him I want to perform at *your* club."

Rex slid his door open, stood on the threshold.

"Yeah, but there's a procedure, you have to audition on Open Mic Monday. Joey, give her the lowdown, won't you?"

"Line up in front of the club early as you can, 9:00 a.m. or so," Joey told her. "At 4:00 o'clock the first ten get numbers and —"

"Sounds *great*." Rosetta cut him off. "I'll do that, be there at dawn — with *bells* on. Pee on the sidewalk if I have to, I'm so *desperate* to get on your stage."

She left amidst clouds of sarcasm. She would rather die than line up with college kids or dentists who thought they could do stand-up comedy.

They gaped after her while Conor smoked efficiently. Rex took the 8x10 from Joey.

"She *try* to look crazy?" he asked.

"Can't look any other way," Conor called. "Truth hurts."

Perri hooted but Rex, bewildered, simply asked, "Ashley coming in today?"

"Any minute, Black."

The phone rang and she picked up. It rang again and Joey picked up. Even Byrne began answering.

Rex closed the glass door.

"Yeah, phones go crazy when our booker comes in," he said. "Ring nonstop like a — a fucking *telethon* or something."

Checking to make sure Carnegie Hall remained, he sat down at his desk — settled in, hands on chair arms, then kicked himself backwards. Conor in half an hour hadn't moved except to attend to his cigarettes. The ashtray held a mound of ash.

"So that's the story," Rex concluded. "And I know all I've talked about is you coming in on a contract basis, couple weeks to clean up violations so the City doesn't close us down, but see, I've got this powder-nosed manager (*if* you know what I mean), she get wind of anything, might sabotage things, walk away with my store."

"Rex, I've *got* a job," Conor said. "I mean, thanks — "

"That fag palace? *C'mon,* Conor. You can do better."

Silence.

"*C'mon,* rock and roll of the *Eighties?*"

Conor sighed — for a smoker, an impressively full-bodied sigh — and mobilized: uncrossed his legs, squashed out his cigarette, stood up looking at Rex through intense blue eyes.

"I'll think about it. Talk it over with my significant O."

"*Terrific!*"

Rex hopped up and escorted him through the bullpen. Perri, Joey and Byrne were telling callers that Ashley was expected soon, call back later. Hold lights flashed.

The office door opened and a tall young woman entered head down, put her bag on the nearest desk and fanned out its mail. She wore a loose top that extended midthigh over black leggings.

"Ash!" said Rex.

"Hey, Rex." Her voice had gravel in it. She was thin, with ash-blonde hair, and when she looked up proved very pretty.

"Ashley Parrish, meet Conor Brennan."

"Hello, Conor Brennan."

"*Hey*-ya."

"Conor's general manager of Poor Richard's Cabaret."

"The Dick? True it's for sale?"

"You hear rumors," said Conor.

"Ashley," Perri called anxiously, "it's Hank."

All business, Ashley sat down and got on the phone while Rex saw Conor to the elevator.

"So let me know?"

"Will do."

The elevator ground distantly.

"Good," said Rex, and fled back into the office.

"How'd it go, Black?" Perri asked.

"Went good. Very sharp. Gave him the full-court press. Wouldn't say, but he's interested."

"That your new manager?" asked Ashley, covering the handset.

"Yeah, if—"

"Think a faggot can handle that crowd? No offense, Joey, no offense, Byrne."

"Hey, this guy's *tough*," said Rex. "Saw him beat up a customer the other night."

A shy knock at the door, and Rex—company face still on—obligingly opened it. The doorman from downstairs stood there blushing, holding out an envelope by one corner.

"Good afternoon, Mr. Black, I hate to—"

"Hey, Reuben, how's it going? That for me?"

Rex took the envelope and opened it.

"Like I say, Mr. Black, I hate to, but you *are* late."

"No problem," Rex said, beaming. "Thanks a lot. Take care

of it today."

He closed the door, balled up the eviction notice, dunked it across the room in Perri's wastebasket.

"*Jerkoff*. Fucking waste of paper."

7.

ROSETTA WENT HOME, called Frank, told him she'd read his play, *loved* it and was free if he cared to come by to discuss it.

Until he showed she worked at her hobby.

Rosetta earned her living as a videographer, manning the camcorder at weddings or bachelorette parties or—her bread and butter—Off-Off-Broadway showcases about to vanish after their four-week runs. For $200 (cash only, please) she consented to be bored (they were always boring) panning from her tripod, zooming in and out, and delivering a dozen videotapes to the broke, rueful producer.

Over time she'd acquired an editing studio's worth of cast-off but serviceable equipment. Its components hulked along the walls of her Jane Street studio apartment, whose furniture as a consequence was shoved to the middle, coffee table on the couch.

Videotape was her recreation as well. As she waited she was working on an old movie on VHS, *Call Northside 777*, borrowed from the Jefferson Market Library. James Stewart plays a newspaper reporter who proves the innocence of a man on Death Row. Rosetta did little until the end, aside from dubbing in her trademark farts and hackings and curses under the breath; restraint as much as honesty was the hallmark of her art.

But in the last scene—where the prisoner is freed, and the young son he's never met runs across the street to be lofted in his arms while Jimmy Stewart simpers—she smoothly overlaid footage from another picture that showed a car hitting a boy with a sickening *thump!* She made Jimmy's gratified smile linger. Thus leached of its treacle, made honest and worthy of being seen by the library-card–carrying public, the film was ready to join her other masterpieces on the shelves.

Frank knocked on her door.

"Oh, hullo, Frank."

"Doesn't your buzzer work?"

"Forgot to tell you. Hope you rang someone else?"

"Someone came in finally. That's why I'm late."

"Are you late? Here's your play. I liked it a lot. But one thing."

He took the chair arm she indicated (the seat held a side table).

"I'm not a gay man, but if I were, and all over town my friends were dying of RH Factor (thought of that last night, isn't it *funny?* RH, Rock Hudson, *get* it?)— I mean, think of the people we both know: Richie at the Dick, John, Ian, Tony—"

"Yes, yes," he said, rushing to forestall the litany. "Every week someone else."

"But that would be my subject, not this bubonic-plague remove. What's *that* about? It's the difference between truth and fairy tale, you see. Bubonic plague's *quaint*. Nothing quaint about AIDS. I know it's a metaphor and all that, but AIDS needs metaphors like we need *it*.

"And truth is the only thing, in stand-up or drama. The

whole art thing is *truth*. And truth hurts."

"Indeed," thought Frank.

"It's the clarity of my vision that makes me seem cruel," Rosetta explained, studying him. "The clearer you see, the crueler you seem. I better get going."

She abruptly pulled off her shirt. Her breasts swarmed wildly before being confined beneath a fresh one. Frank wondered, *Come-on or put-down?* The latter seemed more likely; about what Rosetta would deem deserved by a man who in 1986 New York writes about 1665 London.

"Videos to return, then going up to the Dick for a drink. Went by Rex Black's office earlier, ran into Conor. Is Rex stealing him? Or buying Roland out?"

"Be hard tearing Conor away from the Dick. He loves it."

"Care to come?" Rosetta asked. "Surprise him?"

"No, thanks. May I use your bathroom?"

"In there."

She gathered her tapes—she'd also garnished *Gold Diggers of 1933* with snippets of porn so that its Busby Berkeley routines resolved into the vaginal close-ups their logic demanded—while he went in. When he turned on the light, creatures made for the baseboards. The fixtures, originally white porcelain, were shellacked in amber with a pubic-hair motif. Stench hit him ferociously.

After Frank came out faint from holding his breath, Rosetta volunteered, "A bathroom *should* stink. Why should the bathroom always be the cleanest room in the American home? *Think* about it."

"Didn't say a thing."

They walked out together.

8.

WHEN FRANK GOT IN from Rosetta's, Conor — getting ready to go to work — told him about his meeting with Rex Black.

"I like the guy," he concluded, "but I could never leave the Dick."

"I liked him, too," Frank said.

"Yeah? I'm surprised."

"His kind of energy's the way the world works."

Conor looked amused.

"No, really," Frank insisted. "That determination to worm his way in, get what he wants? A quest as pure as the artist's."

"Whatever."

Conor cabbed uptown, intending to stay at Poor Richard's until the weeknight last call of 2:00 a.m. When he entered, only a dozen regulars were scattered around the front bar. But that Wendy the coatcheck and Justin the bartender and Lorraine waiting tables were buffed and bright-eyed with tension, not to mention that Dooley was playing uptempo, told him Roland was already on the premises.

"*Hey*-ya, Wendy, hold onto this?" he asked, handing over his briefcase. "*Hey*-ya, Justin."

"What'll it be?"

"Um, how 'bout that peppermint schnapps shit?"

Wincing at every sip, Conor stood at the end of the bar, next to the most regular of regulars, Paul and Paolo. Rosetta Stone was sitting at the far end. Conor bought her a drink — that is, gestured towards her when he had Justin's eye. She toasted him in response.

Paolo was talking about his latest decorating client.

"Stone blind, but hates *everything* I bring him. Being blind doesn't stop him from feeling every thread and telling me, 'No, *this* won't work, this is *ugly.*'"

And meanwhile the room found its companionable groove. It was always so when Conor came in. He didn't have to do much to make people feel taken care of, even favored, so expressive was his posture of the joy and freedom *he* felt in being there. His laughter rang out readily, and peppermint schnapps proved surprisingly palatable.

Brat came upstairs. Brat booked the showrooms of both Roland's clubs — the other, in the Village, was called Bar Ditto — and thus was a world power in New York cabaret. He was good, too: However bitter his own outlook, talent didn't get past him unnoticed. Every night he got plowed at one bar or the other, and was half-plowed now.

"There's the bad boy," he said to Conor.

"*Hey*-ya, Brat, what up?"

Brat didn't answer. He sat down beside Rosetta. They were soon laughing thick as thieves.

"What's got into *him*?" Conor asked.

"Some dildo or other," said Paul.

"At the Mineshaft," said Paolo.

Then Roland slithered upstairs. Roland never made noise when he moved. People became aware of his ferret face and toothbrush mustache only when his shaved head metallically caught the light his eyes blinked shy of. He stared at the piano, assessing Dooley's goldfish bowl of tips.

"*Hey*-ya, Roland," said Conor. "You doing the liquor order, or should I?"

Roland moved off.

"Excuse *me*," Conor said.

Like a weasel, Roland in transit could only be glimpsed in stages of his journey, even in a crowd as small as that night's. Conor saw him lift a carafe from a table. Next he was standing where brass rails on the bar set off the waitress station. Next, whispering to Dooley (Dooley picked up the tempo). Next, silhouetted in the showroom door. Then he was gone.

Conor was sipping another schnapps when Roland startled him with a brush of mustache on his cheek.

"Downstairs," he whispered, and vanished.

Conor pretended to shake as he carried drink and cigarette down the steps. Navigating the basement labyrinth of storerooms and sheeted-off dressing rooms, he knocked at a door in the rear.

Roland opened it, his eyes focused on a far horizon as Conor went in and sat down.

"What up, Roland?"

Roland closed the door and finished checking off items on a liquor order. Then he tapped the intercom. "Justin? You and Brat come downstairs, please? Lorraine can fill in."

He sat there not looking at Conor until a knock came at the door. Nudging it open, he told Justin, "Wait there," and left it ajar.

"Well, Conor, I don't know what you expected, but the word's out. I know you don't like me and never have, but I don't give a shit. This is hard for me—*very* hard. Richie took care of me, but now I have to take care of myself. I know you were tight with him, but evidently your loyalty stopped with *him*. And what I need right now is *loyalty*."

His eyes filled and a wash spilled from his nostrils. Sniffing, he grabbed a Kleenex.

"It's always the rats who desert a sinking ship," he went on. "But I'm not going to sink, promise you that. I know the rumor is I'm selling, but no matter *who* might want me to, I'll *never* sell."

Conor patted his shoulder.

"I know," he started, "we both —"

"Richie always said they'd abandon me, *everyone*, as soon as they could, that gay people especially take advantage."

He took an envelope from a drawer and handed it to Conor.

"That's a month's wages, I think that's fair — *more* than fair — and I want you out of here, and don't come back, *ever*."

Time hung fire.

"*Justin!*" squeaked Roland. Justin loomed. Behind him Brat's eyes glittered silver.

Conor drained his glass, said, "Fuck you, Roland," and could barely manage his way up the steps, so shocked was he.

At the top he paused to regroup. Paul and Paolo were gone. He moved aside for Justin to stoop back behind the bar, and again for Lorraine to lift the passthrough and walk out, head held high. Brat rejoined Rosetta, and their heads dipped while Dooley played a wry take on Chopin's funeral march.

As Conor was retrieving his briefcase, Rosetta tapped his shoulder.

"Conor, I had no *idea* Roland would care. Mentioned seeing you at Rex Black's earlier and he, like, *froze*. No idea he'd *think* anything."

"No problem," Conor told her.

He tipped Wendy $10 and found a cab out front.

9.

RIDING DOWNTOWN, CONOR recalled the Saturday Roland woke him up to tell him Richie had died at dawn and he needed help.

He and Frank hurried over to Duane Street. They found Roland weeping in a chair. Richie's body, a shrunken remnant of the college football star's—only its open mouth shockingly large—lay stark and disjointed in bed, one knee gathering the sheet. Conor set about closing his mouth and eyes. The mouth wouldn't close, but shutting his eyes seemed to quiet him some; no one cared for his visible agony just then.

Others came in, Brat and Lorraine among them. The coroner finally arrived, and later two masked and gloved mortuary men who bagged up the body and took it away. Everybody pitched in, pulling on rubber gloves and wiping the place down with bleach.

The bed was a problem. The sheets went down the incinerator chute, but the mattress so vividly chronicled the course of his illness that it seemed more palpably Richie than his abandoned clay. Conor organized a party of pallbearers, and with hands still gloved they bore it giddily down the stairs and over to the nearby Hudson, to the pier where Richie used to take the sun and cruise, and flung it into the water. It bravely crested the wavelets for a few minutes before it sank.

At Christopher Street the cab turned off Seventh Avenue and wound around to Grove Street. In front of Bar Ditto, Conor said, "This is good."

Bar Ditto was a storied old place down eight steps. Passers-by, hearing show tunes sung by a roomful of men who knew the words to every verse, would sometimes squat on the sidewalk to peer inside. They would see a crowd jammed in at tiny tables swaying in unison, singing. Some were drawn in. The rest, baffled, shook their heads and went on their way.

The piano player was taking a break when Conor went in. Behind the bar stood Lita, short, chesty and tough in jeans and plaid.

"*Hey*-ya, Lita."

"Hey, Conor, what'll it be?"

"Let me think, I *need* this drink. Jack Daniel's on the rocks?"

She poured it.

"Thanks, Dolls. I better pay for this one —"

"Don't insult me. FYI, Roland called, said be on the lookout: You're 86'd."

Conor sighed.

"Starting tomorrow, by me. So c'mon, *give*: The fuck you *do*?"

"Bottoms up," he answered.

He looked around as he drank. His first bartending job was right there, as an 18-year-old (the drinking age lower then) whose beauty made everybody nervous. Two years later he was managing it. A few years after that, he helped launch Poor Richard's.

Lita, chin on elbow, was still waiting.

"Oh, Roland got some bee in his bonnet. Guy owns a club

talked to me, Roland found out, thought I was plotting behind his back or something."

"That's *it*?"

"Yep."

"Who told Roland?"

"I'll never tell."

Lita sighed.

"Thanks a lot, fucking it up for the rest of us. Leaves us with that *schmuck* and— I don't even want to think who'll replace you. Brat? Justin?"

"You'll be fine. Roland hardly comes in any more."

"Ready for another? Your money's no good here," she added as he reached for his pocket.

Billy, the other bartender, came over.

"Conor, Roland called again. Might want to be on your way."

"I'm so scared."

More drinks relaxed him to the point of imitating his showdown with The Man: "C'mon, Roland, pretty please, not the deep freeze! Talk to me, *anything* but the deep freeze!" Later still, by request he got up to do his signature singing-bartender number. Parodying a sleazy lounge act's fast medley of *Memories* and *Tomorrow,* he sang, leering,

> *Touch me,*
> *You'll understand what happiness is.*

He was a hit, as always, and celebrated with more Jack Daniel's before kissing everybody goodbye and tipping Lita.

He found himself at the 24-hour deli around the corner— usually his last stop, for he believed in going to bed on a full stomach when drinking—where he stood for five minutes gravely inspecting the salad bar. He bought a raspberry FrozFruit and a pack of Marlboros.

Nibbling at the FrozFruit, he moved down the street. Conor

kept as dispassionate a watch on his needs as a building engineer on his boiler, who, when the ball-cock needs venting, vents it. He flipped the stick into the gutter and, halting, tore open the cigarettes, fluttering cellophane into the air. With two authoritative taps he shot a cigarette into his fingers and lighted it, closing an eye to reduce the two flames he saw to one, and walked onwards.

On Hudson Street he flicked the butt at the curb and went into a bookstore. He paged through magazines. Naked men of gratifying endowment stared back. Ignoring the other browsers, and buying no magazines, he nonetheless paid the clerk, bundled his wallet into his briefcase and, exchanging it for a claim tag, passed through a turnstile and curtain into a gamy, profoundly dark chamber of sighs, grunts, whispers and urgings.

Stumbling past several shapes of cloth and flesh, he walked full on into something that would not give way and stood still as hands groped him. He assisted with belt and buttons, then simply fought to keep his balance as a man irresistibly pushed his lips the length of his cock.

He lasted as long as he could while the man worried his crotch like a pitbull, then pulled him off so as to flurry himself. He gave a preliminary moan but didn't mean to cry out. But he did cry out as he daubed the man with semen.

While the other then agitated himself to loud climax Conor aimed him tidily aside with, "Careful, Cowboy." Then, restoring his clothing, he whispered with distaste, "You really got into it."

He reclaimed his briefcase and hailed a cab.

Home again, he used the john, washed his face, took the two Tylenol he swore by and clambered up to bed.

Waking up, Frank stretched into him, breathing in aromas of cigarettes, liquor and something faintly, alluringly sexual.

He put his hand to Conor's chest. It stealthily descended.

This had worked a time or two.

Conor lifted it off. "Move over, Dolls," he said.

"Make me."

"Not tonight, I'm tired."

"You'll feel better."

"You only want one thing," Conor said.

Frank was perplexed that the one thing was so seldom granted. And all Conor offered as to why was, "I don't know." Frank's theory was that his parents' and Richie's deaths had unsettled him. They weren't having problems that he knew about. He hoped things would improve with time, and knew his job meanwhile was to be supportive.

He didn't know that Conor was one of those proud gay men whose accepted task it is to dig up a new body every time he wants sex. What makes New York so great for the proud gay man—who holds that to be inhibited from promiscuity is to internalize the larger society's homophobia—is that he can't go three blocks without finding a willing, adequately buff body. It was Frank's misfortune to take sex personally; sex with a stranger seemed like nothing at all.

Conor warned him after their first night together, "Having sex with you is like making love." But Frank didn't, couldn't, take heed. When they did have sex, just when Frank's excitement became urgent and global, Conor would reclaim his own genitals and leave him to shift for himself.

"Conor, is anything—?"

"Guess what? Roland fired me."

This diverted Frank, but Conor didn't want to talk about that, either.

Even with sex not a possibility, still they slept jammed into each other, contour pressed to yielding contour, and if one strayed, the other in his sleep followed.

10.

UNTIL A FEW WEEKS earlier, Rex had been butting his head against a wall with his idea of taking the Gag Reflex public. He conceived the notion while still Germano's partner (he didn't share it), but becoming sole owner won him no automatic entrée through that wall. It needed an underwriter to carry the company to market.

He worked every contact trying to get meetings with Allen & Co. and other investment houses that bankrolled the entertainment industry. And once or twice he got them — sat down with guys in serious suits who, amused at indulging a nightclub owner, traded stories of their stoned and long-haired youth before perfunctorily flipping through his business plan as he explained, with all the sincerity he could muster, how comedy was the rock and roll of the Eighties. They didn't get it. They wished him luck.

He was reduced to messengering copies of his plan around town with cover letters to his own eyes pathetic: "So-and-so suggested that I tell you about an opportunity. . . "

Until the day Joe D. told him whom to call.

"Sick and tired of your not paying rent," he growled over

the telephone. "You do business, where does it *go?*"

Rex tried to explain his nut, the necessity of an office suite on 57th Street, of appearing to be already rolling in the dough he needed to accomplish his IPO.

"Don't see why you make it so difficult, Rex."

"I should just call Goldman Sachs, right, see if Mr. Sachs or maybe Mr. Goldman wants to catch a show? Joe, you don't know how hard just getting *through* to these guys—"

"Maple Tree Investors could set you up."

"Wait, know anyone at Allen & Company?"

"Maple Tree. Ask for Sigmund Brewster. Old friend," he started to say, but amended it: "Old *client* of mine. I want my rent, *capisc'?*"

Rex hated it when Joe D. went Sicilian on him.

But he did call Maple Tree Investors and ask for Sigmund Brewster, and got through in about two seconds.

"Rex Black! When're you coming downtown?"

It seemed that, having heard about his plans from their mutual friend, Sigmund Brewster wanted nothing so much as to receive Rex at Maple Tree's offices high off Broad Street. They agreed on lunch the following day.

"Oh, and bring some numbers with you, give me an idea what you did last few quarters, that kind of shit. Projections a year from now, five years. Nothing fancy."

For such state occasions, Rex hired his friend Ginger's white stretch Lincoln Continental. Ginger had a nice business going, and Rex intended to hit him up for a private placement—give him the privilege of buying a chunk of stock *before* the IPO. After he hinted as much, Ginger shut up about his outstanding bill.

Ginger released him, precisely on time, to Broad Street's teeming, shadowed sidewalk far beneath a jagged escape of blue. Rex entered a dark lane too narrow for vehicles where store windows were lighted in midday, and found the lamplighted entrance to Maple Tree's building. A handsome young man in pinstripes darted forward.

"Mr. Black?

"Yes?"

"I'm Noah Winsocket," the young man said, brushing back an errant shock of hair. "Mr. Brewster's upstairs."

Noah led him through a grand, old-time lobby, marble columns marching beneath chandeliers to a bank of gilt-fronted elevators. Maple Tree's exclusive cab, manned by a uniformed dwarf on a stool, whisked them express to the top floor.

"Maple Tree," said the dwarf. "Watch your step."

"Thanks, Manny," Noah murmured, and escorted Rex into a sky-lighted reception area featuring an enormous Persian rug and a colonnade. He introduced Barbie, her chest tented, her face like an angel's. Behind her desk stood bronze doors cast in images of industry: There a man turned a wrench, here an oil derrick lent geometry to a pastoral scene.

"Mr. Brewster hopes you like your steak rare?" Barbie asked.

"Sure," said Rex. She evinced joy, and must also have pressed a button, because a crude-looking man moving on stumpy legs threw open both sides of the bronze doors.

"Rex Black!" he said. "Siggy Brewster!"

His hand was large and grasping, warm as though he'd snatched it from a litter of kittens. Only his smile saved his oversized head from being scary.

"Mr. Brews—"

"*Siggy*. Like horseradish? Horseradish, Barbie. Thanks, Noah."

Noah receded with inclined head, and Siggy showed Rex into his enormous paneled office. Windows claimed New York

Harbor, New Jersey, Staten Island, too. The air conditioning was fierce for October. Siggy walked to a grouping of chairs beside a burning fireplace. Rex could see that his suit was costly, and yet its mirror-polish hung wrong.

"Siggy, I must say, I'm impressed."

"By—? Oh, by *this*? Give me a break, had a decent kitchen, wouldn't have to send out. No reason why we couldn't get better space in the suburbs. In fact, looked behind Paramus Mall last week, but my hands are tied. Our mutual friend can tell you: *Tradition*. In a little family business like mine, that's something you don't buck."

"See Joe often?"

"Nearly sawed off my head just last week."

Rex felt his testicles lift into his body as Siggy, frowning, drew a hand across his throat.

"Take a load off, Rex. Can tell by shaking your hand I'm going to like doing business with you." They sat down, Rex in a tapestried wingchair, Siggy in a green leather English porter's chair cowled against drafty London evenings. "So tell me, what's going on?"

As he bemusedly listened to Rex's pitch, Siggy stared deep into the tongues of orange and yellow flame licking at oak logs. Occasionally he looked up from the shadows, dark eyes and thick brows melting into empathetic blackness in the middle of his face.

"This is what I love to hear," he remarked comfortably. "*Beautiful*. Nothing the market likes better than a young man with a dream and a brand name: *The Gag Reflex!* Combine that with the zeitgeist—that how you say it? *Zeitgeist!*—and the market will salute!

"Rex, telling you, have to go back to Lew Wasserman to find your vision of integrating an entertainment company." Adjusting the hang of his balls, he asked, "Bring those numbers? Let's give 'em the Wasserman test."

Rex handed over his business plan.

"Whole point of this is we're already doing better—"

Holding the pages at arm's length, Siggy winked him to silence.

"Fine, fine, nothing here to be ashamed of. Hungry? Let's eat. *Hey!*" he called, snapping his fingers. A gray-bearded waiter appeared and unfolded TV trays, one painted with Dumbo for Rex, the other lurid with Donald Duck for Siggy. He laid places, served salads and steaks, and carried off the business plan.

"Apologies," said Siggy. "The Palm sends this down, choice is nuke it or not, and I choose *not*. Don't trust those things. So if they're cold—"

But they weren't. The steaks were hot and delicious.

"Joe says you have a wife? *Perri?* Pretty name. Have to meet mine. *Mandy*. We live in Bedford, she doesn't care for the city, which in one way— Two daughters. Teens. How do people *do* it? Joe says send 'em to the old country, let his cousins whip sense into 'em, but Mandy claims Miss Porter's up to it. *I* don't know."

No business was discussed during the more serious affair of cutting tender red meat. But when he finally clattered down his knife and fork, and the waiter cleared and served hot fudge sundaes, Siggy yelled, "*Berger! Enfield! Williams!*"

Three young men—possibly Noah Winsocket's frat brothers—came in, each holding a fresh copy of Rex's business plan.

"So, guys, take a look?"

They nodded.

"*And?*"

"We can do it, Mr. B."

"Real possibilities, Mr. B."

But the third said, *"Thin,* Mr. B. Few years of better numbers, maybe, but on these we'd be crazy to have anything to do with it."

Siggy opened his hands in pain.

"This what I pay you for, Williams?"

"Just saying —"

"You can go." Williams withdrew in shame. After affably nodding the other two out, Siggy turned to his guest. "Thing of it is, Rex, we're dealing with intangibles here. You got no factories, no inventory, just a store lease and a name, and that makes the young fogies nervous. But the economy's moving on, it's a new, intangible world.

"You know, people run down what we do here, whole term of art's a fucking putdown: *penny stocks.* But number one, say Maple Tree brings you to market at five bucks, where's the penny? So not fair. But price you at $35? *Sixty?* Who the fuck's going to *buy?"*

Working to his feet, Siggy went behind his desk. Its top was clean but for two telephones, a carved jade knife and a lamp whose parchment shade was painted with clipper ships. Summoning Rex, he swept his arm across the windows.

"The big boys — Merrill Lynch is right over there, Goldman's behind that, Morgan we can't see — the *big boys* ignore us, but a few years from now, they're going to look over hear and be surprised as shit.

"Rex," he asked, "we got a deal?"

"Deal, Siggy."

They shook hands.

"My man Harshaw'll work it up, send it over. Leave everything to me: Your job is to rain down the profits! Hey, and I want to come see a show!"

"Any time."

Siggy pressed a button and Noah Winsocket materialized.

"Noah, Mr. Black will have my car this afternoon."

"Hey, thanks," murmured Rex, "but my driver's waiting."

"Shame, I got the only Daimler limousine in town. Same as the Queen Mother's? People think the royal family uses Rolls-Royces, which for errands they do, but otherwise Rolls-Royces aren't good enough for them, or for me.

"Hey, want to see the shark tank? Show him, Noah. Rex: *Peace.*"

And on the way out, in a region of plush and quiet offices, Noah opened the door to Pandemonium, a large room filled with young men screaming into telephones before banks of glowing green or gold screens.

"Our trading floor," Noah said. "Mr. Brewster calls it the shark tank."

Rex nodded, hugely impressed.

Bidding Noah goodbye by lamplight and walking into Broad Street, Rex saw an elegant monstrosity at the curb. The driver, seven feet of ebony, was polishing its swooping fender. Then Ginger swung across with his glitzy length of flash, and Rex got in.

Two hours in Siggy's inner sanctum had changed him. For the first time he saw the vulgarity of the Lincoln's interior, with its curvy chrome bits and shiny wood appliqués. But as they rolled, people were looking at him enviously.

"They want what I have," Rex meditated, "but what I want is what *Siggy* has — *more* than Siggy!

"That's why we're the greatest nation on earth," he suddenly realized. "We *want* the most! The way building the pyramids organized the Egyptians? *Wanting* organizes us!

"The American dream's about wanting more of what you *do* have and everything you *don't* — about that emptiness that inspires you to go after your dream — to find a new top to the pyramid! Appetite's our principle! We pledge allegiance to filling up our emptiness!

"That finger down the throat of the Gag Reflex? Logo for the zeitgeist! Purges you, freshens your appetite, leaves you empty and wanting more! 'I *want*, therefore I *am!*' 'I *want* it, so I'm *entitled!*'

"But so long as *I* want more than *they* do, they're *mine!*"

Speeding up the West Side Highway, Rex watched the skyline rapidly swapping skyscrapers.

"I'm *in!*" he was thinking. "I'm *in!* I'm *in!*"

11.

IN HIS FIRST DAYS OF unemployment Conor amused himself devising another Halloween Parade masterpiece, a Moonie wedding for a dozen brides and dozen grooms. Himself, Frank and their fellow brides he arrayed in gowns confected at his sewing machine out of $1-a-yard fabric and 50¢-a-yard netting from Brooklyn's Fulton Street Mall, the fetching ensembles complete unto wigs, lipstick, makeup and balloon breasts. The grooms bound their breasts and wore tuxedos beneath false beards and extravagant mascara mustachios.

The solemn, starry-eyed procession caused a sensation. Its own finger-snapping doo-wop wedding march spontaneously accompanied it:

> *Going to the chapel*
> *and we're gonna get married . . .*

But it caused some confusion, too. One 12-year-old boy set out to crack the code. He ran down the line chanting, "That's a man, that's a woman, that's a man," until he got to, "That's a — That's a —" and ran off, lost.

Then a week of watching HBO to the drizzles of November

wore Conor down. Joey took his defeated call accepting Rex's offer.

"Just to bring it up to code, Joey."

"In the end I bet —"

"Have my doubts about Rex."

"Rex is *awesome*, Conor. Just have to make sure he's on your side."

"Exactly."

"Hey, work for him and he's with you."

"Frank's going to help."

"Super!"

Frank's offer came when Conor unwarily said, "I'd ask you to pitch in, weren't so busy."

"I *will*."

"But your play? Your job?"

"Play's on the back burner, Rosetta pointed out some problems. And TIME's only Saturday night."

The morning they began, Joey met them in front of the club, waiting beside a rented dumpster on a sidewalk as thickly blotched with chewing gum as the one outside Bloomingdale's. In those days the neighborhood was still more Yorkville than Upper East Side: More tenements crowded fewer towers, and German restaurants outnumbered boutiques.

Inside, they sniffed a stale compound of liquor, tobacco, sewage and flop sweat, exhalations that appalled Frank but piqued Conor and made him feel at home. "*Um, um, um,*" he said.

Nightclubs look ghastly outside of business hours. The moment of transition at the Dick always came long after last call, when a warning was shouted and, faces averted or not, the work lights went up, replacing the club's muted scheme with a subway glare that blanched beauties into zombies and made the room look like a junk shop.

The Gag Reflex by daylight was even drearier.

First they moved the rickety tables and chairs off the showroom's ragged carpeting, mashed to the texture of dirt and streaked with stringy duct tape that served more to mark than to mask the holes. Tying cloths over their faces like outlaws, they pulled it up at the walls, heaving fountains and spews of soil into the air, rolled it up and dragged it out the door into the dumpster. They swept the skinned floor clear of matchbooks, butts, spoons, shards of glass, toothpicks, bottle caps and pennies. Conor called out at an area spilled with powder, but Joey, tasting a frosted pinky, pronounced it baking soda at best.

"Wouldn't a bare floor be better?" Frank asked.

"Not this one," Joey said. "Cost more to fix up than to carpet."

"And the noise," Conor put in. "But remember, it's not the look of the room, it's the magic onstage."

"Rex says his reason for not renovating?" said Joey. "Might hurt the magic."

"*Sheesh.*"

They maneuvered the new carpeting inside, unrolled it past the stage and, pulling it tight, shot in dozens of screws. Laying it had the satisfying effect of slapping down a coat of paint.

"That's better," said Conor, swabbing up his sweat and lighting a cigarette. His eyes happened to stray upwards, to a ceiling tufted with white canvas like a gigantic, upside-down mattress. "Fuck going on up *there*, Joey?"

"Asbestos. But it's legal, sealed like that."

For lunch they went next door to the Yellow Parrot, a diner crowded with lemon-colored booths beneath a chalkboard commanding *Stop the madness!*

"This is where the comedians come," Joey told them. "Where else, on what we pay them?"

"How much *do* they get?" Conor asked.

"During the week, five bucks a set—cabfare, we call it—plus their drinks. On weekends, the set shows, $20. Hey," Joey added, seeing their surprise, "they don't get more *anywhere*."

"Oh shit," said Conor, looking out the window.

An old man shuffling past, wheeling an oxygen tank from which tubes coursed to his nose, had stopped and with a strain scary to see was trying to turn around.

Standing up, Frank saw that the leashes of the man's Yorkies were entwining his legs. He dashed outdoors and—braving three sets of snapping jaws—unwound them.

"Wow, really got tangled up there," he said.

"Thank you, young man," the man said firmly in a large voice.

"How far are you going?"

"Just here." He pointed to the doorway beside the club.

"Need help with the stairs?"

"No, thanks, I just take my time."

Joey was cracking up when Frank returned.

"Old geezer lives upstairs. Still a few tenants. Must take him all morning to get down, the afternoon to get up again."

"Who owns the building?" asked Conor.

"A Mafioso," Joey said, suddenly serious.

"Joe D.?"

"The fuck you know *that*?"

"Called the other night."

"Yeah, he's an enforcer with the Gambinos. They say Germano had a sitdown once and shat his pants—literally."

"What's he got on Rex?"

"Oh, *nothing*: Rex owes him like half a year's back rent, that's all. Joe D.'s got him by the *balls*."

After lunch Joey left for the office. Back in the showroom Conor stared at the ceiling.

"This should be easy, Dolls," he said. "Come on."

At a hardware store they rented a blower and bought five gallons of flat black paint. After two hours of a blacking campaign, nothing of the ceiling could be seen: It was densely invisible.

"Very tasteful," said Conor. He went slowly round the room, giving it a good look. The paneled walls were decorated with odd old stuff: here vaudeville posters, there a collection of Laurel and Hardy plates. "What a dump. But in its way it could be nice."

"I *knew* it," said Frank. "It's a challenge."

"Holding up, Dolls? Or had enough?"

"No, I'm fine. It's fun." To Conor's skeptical look he added, "Fun doing something with results you can see. Fun working with *you*."

"Feel like spending the evening downstairs?"

"Love to."

For hours they spackled joint compound into rock walls (rodent menace, claimed the City), when it dried and shrank cramming in more. They cleared piles of trash: chairs broken beyond repair but stashed against a better day, broken glasses, rotting tablecloths.

From overhead came a succession of rhythms. A woman began answering the phone that had been ringing all day. Later came band practice—a muffled trio of piano, drums and guitar. Waitresses set up their stations with quick footsteps that made floorboards chatter. Later came the heavier impress of customers tramping to their tables. The show began, coming through the floor with a dreamlike quality. The band played, an amplified voice took over and the audience began to produce a distant, threatening, unhappy sound: *Laughter*.

Coral tripped down the steps and was scared out of her wits—and saddened—by the apparition of Conor and Frank carrying garbage bags past.

"Don't know how you stand it, Coral. What a pigsty."

"Isn't it *awful?*"

In the office she pored over invoices and made calls, careful to close the door before dropping into a whine.

For Frank, working with Conor all afternoon and evening, *helping* him, consecrated the day. He never felt more in love than when they were whisking the undersides of floor joists together, spiders falling into their faces.

It gave him an idea, one he waited to voice until after they brought back slices and sodas from the corner pizzeria and, sitting beside the sidewalk chute, ate as customers hurried inside past the retching neon. He foresaw Conor's taking the manager's job and then meeting with frustration owing to his new boss's shifting focus and desperate need for cash.

When the slices were gone, their cans drained and Conor was peaceably dragging on a cigarette, Frank suggested, "Maybe I could work for Rex, too?"

"*Too?* You're assuming?"

"I don't mean here: In the office? I'd watch your back. We'd be a team."

Conor took a deep breath. He looked burdened. Reach for him and his reflex was to withdraw.

"Let's get back to work, Dolls," he said. "Inspector comes in two weeks."

12.

PERRI WAS FEELING DOWN, queasy with what she hoped wasn't just a tummyache. From her desk the office looked very tired. The gold records resembled tin-can lids. The airshaft implied that life's but grime and squalor.

And in front of her rose a daunting pile of bills, presented by letters whose vocabulary of *overlooked* and *regret* did nothing to palliate their wounding lack of faith. She lighted a candle, but instead of feeling refreshed by its scent felt a vague new sense of oppression. She pinched the flame out.

Then her ob/gyn called and confirmed that she was pregnant. Gold disks flashing in the sun, she hugged herself, turned off her music and got up to tell Rex.

She slid open his door to "The *fuck*, Germano, serve one Bud without that fucking affidavit, City'll close me the fuck *down!*"

Out the window Perri saw a woman on 57th Street pushing a stroller that held a bundle of blue. With a tug she felt herself to be that child's mother — *every* child's mother. It was a large, beautiful feeling.

Rex jammed the phone to his chest.

"*What?*"

Perri smiled enigmatically.

"*Fuck* you, Germano, call you back." He punched the phone into its cradle. "Perri, what *is* it?"

"Dr. Liebman called, Black: I'm pregnant."

"*No!*"

Taking her hands, he kissed her, sat her down solicitously. They made plans to celebrate at dinner, and agreed to keep the news quiet until she started showing.

He did venture one nervous question.

"Still with me? 'Cause I need you more than ever, Perri, but you're going to be busy blowing up your belly."

"*Black!*" she laughed. She reassured him.

They rejoiced until it was time to start the meeting. Wednesday was meeting day, when Ashley came in early and Perri ordered Thai food and iced tea from downstairs. She herself stuck to her macrobiotic diet, bringing to the conference table a multitude of plastic containers, tiny forkfuls of whose contents she chewed so assiduously she could seldom contribute to the discussion.

But today she pushed aside what she'd brought and dug into the Thai chicken along with Rex, Ashley and Joey.

"Perri, you're *glowing*," said Ashley. "What happened? Meet someone?"

Rex smirked. Perri looked surprised.

"New conditioner, that's all."

"What's it called, *Maternal Glow?*"

"*Avocado* something. For shine."

First on the agenda was the City's upcoming club inspection.

"This time we'll pass," Rex said. "See that ceiling? *Amazing.* And you could *eat* off the cellar floor. We pass, I say we lock up Conor fast."

No one disagreed.

When Perri used the bathroom, Ashley rasped, "So what is it with her? Preggers?"

"Yeah," said Rex. "Matter of fact, she is."

Perri emerged to hugs.

"Perri, that's *wonderful*."

"Congratulations!"

"Oh great, Black," she said, sitting down. "You told them?"

"Family gets to know."

"Family?"

"Perri, anyone who works for me is *family*. That's the only basis I'll go ahead on."

She didn't mind. Joey she loved, and she and Ashley were becoming closer. Her initial aversion she attributed to Ashley's rarefied background, but you can't blame someone for her ancestors, and by now she was Ashley's confidante in her endless crushes on comedians.

"When's it due?" Joey asked.

"July 1st."

"Boy or girl?"

"Don't know yet."

Afterwards Byrne went to lunch, and Perri and Rex adjourned behind glass.

"Now the real meeting begins," Ashley remarked.

"So cool," said Joey from his doorway. "A kid!"

"Rex is such a jerk. They should wait."

"For the IPO?"

"To see where they are in a few years."

"Someone woke up on the wrong side of bed."

"My fucking roommate," said Ashley. "As per fucking usual."

Joey could only sympathize. Perhaps elsewhere in the country someone with the wrong roommate can move, but that's no easy option where one is condemned or ordained to the apartment Manhattan's cosmic real-estate lottery has dealt out. Ashley might be rich, but as with most rich people Joey knew, her money stayed well out of sight.

"What time she stagger in?"

"Three a.m., *tanked*. First I hear the mutterings in the hall— amazed the neighbors don't complain. 'Where's 30-F? This 30-F?' Someone's door rattles. 'No, not it. Try this one. Yeah, *feels* like 30-F, but why won't the key turn? Hey, Ash! Fucking *bitch*, you in there?'"

Joey laughed.

"Think it's funny? I suppose I should go get her, but she's not putting me in the mood, you know? But eventually she figures it out, door swings open, pulls her inside. Hair's a rat's nest, makeup's smeared, top's slipped down her shoulder. '*Cunt*, why'd you lock me out? The fuck, I got *work* tomorrow, thank you very much.'"

"What you do?"

"Ignored her. She bangs into everything, leaves a trail of water, but finally goes to bed and I can get some sleep."

"Don't know how you put up with it," said Joey. "Anyway, after the IPO you can move."

"Yeah?"

"The stock options, Ashley!"

"Really think people are going to buy stock in that hole?"

Joey was taken aback.

"Hey, comedy's the rock and roll—"

"—of the Fifties, or something. I know, I know. Powder your nose?"

It was rhetorical; she knew Joey was too chickenshit to do cocaine with Rex in the office. She went into the bathroom and ran the faucet while doing quick lines. Through the door to Rex's office she heard monotonous, somehow conspiratorial conversation. Back at her desk she started a cigarette.

Perri came into the bullpen.

"Good meeting, guys. Any messages?"

As she sat down, her hair brushed a pentangle hanging above her desk.

"*Ouch!* Ashley, meant to ask, would you like this? You've admired it—"

Bearing the trophy away, Ashley affixed it to her lamp. Perri struck a match to relight her candle but, seeing Ashley eye it, made a gift of it also.

Ashley went to the club every night and usually stayed, as she put it, until the last comedian died. But that evening her head was somehow too full of Perri's news to let her follow what was happening onstage, as Gilbert Gottfried, Gary Lazer, Lou DiMaggio, Stu Trivax, Randy Credico, Carol Leifer and a teenager named Chris Rock alternately convulsed and puzzled the room. She sat at her table in the corner nearest the front bar, drinking until she had to close one eye, then went for a bite to the Yellow Parrot with comedians who spat food in high arcs as they desperately tried to top one another.

She returned to the club, but abruptly went home.

"Can't stand it tonight, Sly," she said. "It's getting old. Or maybe I am."

"Yeah, like really," Sly said agreeably. Ashley was 28.

She lived a long block over, on York, high in Mansion Towers. Upstairs she unlocked her door and, nudging it open, listened warily. No one home. Good. She turned lights on and poured herself a nightcap.

Her bedroom and the living room shared a terrace. The door to it from the bedroom was blocked with planters and a loveseat. But from the living room she could get there. She hated it, but sometimes it had its Sirens, and tonight they were calling.

First she slid the door open for ventilation. The cold air cutting into the warm apartment felt good, but the blowing curtains put her in mind of a giant waving his arms, so she pulled them back.

Then she stood on the threshold, sipping her drink and looking westward at the towers silently vying with one another. At such heights few close their curtains; everyone lives on display in a convention of mutual invisibility. But most apartments were dark, save for the blue aura of television blowing erratically through.

Taking a step into the clear air, she was enveloped by New York's hum and buzz, a madman's inner voice that never stops. Putting her glass down, gingerly taking baby steps, she arrived at the railing, both hands smacking it: *Safe.* Fingers gripping the pipe so tightly they squashed her nails white, her head lolled over. Her eyes enlarged at the street's lighted blackness, and she tried mightily to keep from slipping over. But blackness pried and pulled at every finger, and she felt the building tilt, the terrace sink away, and the pavement, crawling with yellow things, loom close—very close. She counted the seconds her screaming fall would take, and realized she would have to take a breath halfway down.

Closing her eyes and crouching, she let go, crawled inside, slid the door shut and, breathing hard, sat against it.

Rather than retrieve her drink from the balcony, she made herself a fresh one.

13.

CRÊPE-PAPER TURKEYS DANGLED over Rex and Conor at the Gag Reflex's bar as laughter cascaded out of the showroom. Around them milled comedians. Those who'd already performed were drinking in relief or anger and looking for someone to share a cab to the next club. Those yet to go on were drinking and trying to make themselves visible. Thanksgiving was just over. The building inspector, come and gone, had reluctantly conceded the club to be up to code.

Conor was there not to celebrate, but to cash his and Frank's checks from the clean-up. They'd bounced, and Rex said to bring them by, Coral would cash them out of the register.

"Conor, place looks *sensational*," Rex told him. He downed the last of his tonic. By the time the glass returned to the copper bartop, Sly was poised to pour a fresh one. "So: Want to work for me? Manage my club?"

Conor stared at his foul liqueur. "Yeah, I guess."

"You and your friend's checks bouncing, that was a mistake. Cleared that up, right?"

"Rex, I got to know every square inch of this place. Not a

pretty picture."

"Tell me about it!"

"I take over, it's on the basis you'll renovate."

"What'cha need?"

"Tables. Chairs. Lights. Sound system. New a/c—I hear horror stories. Decent bathrooms. New sodaguns. Smoke eaters. Beerbox. Everything any neighborhood bar needs, let alone your national showplace."

"You *got* it. After the IPO, we'll shut down, do it right."

"So what kind of salary we talking?"

Not meaning to, Rex stiffened.

"Show me yours."

"Thousand a week?"

"Fuck you!" Rex looked relieved: back on his home turf. "Not going to happen. Can't afford that, Conor—nowhere *near*. Would if I could, *you* know that. Going to make you rich, but can't do it I go bust first. We'll raise you fast as we can, I promise."

They finally agreed on $600 a week. Conor wouldn't have any bar shifts, and forgoing those tips meant he wouldn't actually take home more than from Poor Richard's, but retiring from behind the bar was a step up, too. They shook hands and Conor left.

The next time Coral passed, Rex called, "Coral! Talk to you a minute?"

She knew exactly what was coming, and she got it. Rex left with bright-faced waves at everyone.

He wanted to leave no time for factions to form in jumping Conor from hole-filler to general manager, so called a staff meeting the next day. Conor came to 57th Street, and at 5:00 o'clock Ginger's stretch arrived and everybody piled in. Rex and Perri took the forward-facing seat, Conor, Joey and Ashley squeezed shoulder-to-shoulder opposite, and the limo looped uptown beneath Central Park's bare branches.

"So Ashley, how's the roommate from hell?" asked Perri, obeying the law that turns conversation outside the office personal.

"Oh God," said Ashley, "now she's got herself a boyfriend."

Conor lent half an ear, the other half going to Rex, who was on the car phone with Chester, his accountant.

"Who is he?" asked Perri. "What's he like?"

"Real jerk. Married, for starters. Has his own company — shoeshine and a smile. And the wife? Preggers."

"I'm on tenterhooks," Perri said. "Your roommate's better than a soap opera."

"What a lowlife," said Joey. "What's in it for *her?*"

"Hot sex. Oh, plus she's in *love.* Going to take him away from wifey and *marry* him."

"Time you put *her* out on the street," said Perri.

"Yeah, really," said Joey.

"I don't know," Ashley said. She rubbed a malachite disk between her fingers — Perri's old worry-bead, a recent gift. "Wife doesn't really know him, so how's that going to end, anyway?"

"None of her business," Perri said. "Tell her hands off."

"Like I can tell her anything."

"Bring her by the club," Joey suggested. "Introduce her."

"That dump? Wouldn't be caught dead."

At 72nd Street Ginger crossed to First Avenue.

"Yeah, yeah, my point exactly," Rex was saying. "Strong quarters back to back for the prospectus . . . Yeah . . . Yeah . . ." He shot a look at Conor and dropped his voice. "Chester, that's *settled*, had a talk with him . . . What do I mean, 'had a talk with him'? Had a *talk.* Need a strong manager in there —" His voice dropped again. Conor thought he heard, "Gave my *word,* Chester, 600, *shook* on it . . . *No,* my general manager's not tending bar: Let's presume a little *class.*"

They pulled up in front of the club. Anxious faces peered out and retreated. When Ginger came around and opened the door, and Conor helped Perri out, Rex was whispering, "And if he *walks?* With the other one already *fired?*"

Conor wondered if anyone was at the other end of the line.

"Black, get off the phone, we're waiting."

Out loud Rex said, "OK, Chester, be it on your head." Hanging up, he patted the place next to him. "Conor, mind? Sit with me a minute. Rest of you, *go.*"

Conor sat down again, in the facing seat.

"What up, Rex?"

"Just had a chat with my accountant. Know I said I'd start you at 600, but turns out I *can't.* Going to have to trust me, start at *five.* Where do I get the fucking nerve?"

"How much was Coral making?"

"Look, Germano had things on a totally fucking unreal basis, paid people completely out of whack with what the place brings in. He could afford to—three Number One hits in a row? To *him* this club's like what's in my pocket is to *me.*" Squirming his hip out, Rex jammed a hand into his pants and brought it out jangling with change that, when he opened his fingers, sprang over the car. *"Fuck!"*

He plucked coins up from where they fell on the carpeting, but some slid into the crack of the seat, so, kneeling, he plunged his hand after them, Armani sleeves bunching between the seat's leather cheeks. He pulled his hand out. It held two quarters and an empty Ramses package.

"Shit! Ginger!"

"Rex, you paid Coral 750 a week." Conor had it from Joey.

"*Germano* paid that. But now's the time to get *our* relationship on a solid basis. Won't get another chance. Go

with me on this one, your raises will come so thick and fast –
and stock options! Did I mention the *stock* options? Conor, I'm
going to make you *rich!"*

"Five hundred? Club this size? Don't think so."

Ginger got back behind the wheel and discreetly kept an
eye on his passengers in the mirror.

"OK, Conor, do what you got to do. *Sheesh,* my hands are
tied here. Chester knows, fucking name of the game is, 'How
does the Street see it?' If at *500* the Street *likes* it, I can sell my
stock, roll out nationally, but at *600* I'm fucking well *fooling*
myself –" Color drained to the edges of his face. "Don't think
I'm *winging* it? 'Cause I'm fucking well *not*: It's in black and
white, I sweated *blood* writing the business plan that's
Chester's bible, that caught the eye of Maple Tree Investors
and impressed Harshaw & Crowfoot, top securities lawyers –
Any idea what *they* cost? Old Man Harshaw bills at 350 bucks
a fucking hour! Take a meeting with him, I don't even ask *How
are ya?* 'cause that's ten bucks right there!

"Know how much fucking legal work's involved in taking
a company public? Ever hear of blue-sky registration? Register
in every state we might ever want to do business in! And
trademark shit? Don't come cheap, national search, then publish
and protect!

"And who you think writes the fucking prospectus?
Hundred pages laying out everything we got – every mole,
every pimple, every steamy centerfold pose we can come up
with, baby, at 350 *per.*

"Think I'm making this up? Come by the office, look at the
fucking business plan! Says the manager gets *500 a week*. Yeah,
right after the meeting, you're coming back with me and
sitting down, I don't care it takes all night, going to read it till
you say, '*Fuck* me, I'm in on the ground floor of what's going
to make me *rich!'"*

Rex sat forward giving Conor the most open look he was capable of.

"First I have to will it into existence. I'll do it, but meanwhile any prick can say, 'Look, the emperor's naked!' Juggling here, Conor. Ball falls on the floor, I have to pretend it's still flying till I can kick it up again. Trust me, all this has taught me a lot about myself. A man never knows himself until he's signed his own paycheck."

"Pay me the 600 we agreed and you're on," Conor told him. "Can't do that, I'll cab home right now, no hard feelings."

Rex capitulated with a handshake.

"Just fuck me in the ass, Conor, that couldn't hurt so bad. But give me my two quarters."

"Other hand?"

"*Fiscal* quarters. Show 'em how the club blooms under me, the Street'll give us our money and we'll go across the fucking *country*."

"You got it, Rex," said Conor.

Inside, Sly asked Perri, "Hear about Coral?"

"He didn't *want* to—" Perri began.

"No, her new job? Back with Germano, to work on Tintinella's videos. Thousand a week. One phone call."

Perri's face went prim.

"So happy for her. Things work out, don't they? Everybody here?"

"Everyone but Rex," said Sly. They looked out and saw him reaching into the seat, ass in the air. After a minute Conor smiled and leaned back, then searched for his briefcase and got out. Rex followed, adjusting his cuffs and smoothing his hair.

"Rex looks like he just had sex," said Ashley.

Coming inside, Rex brightened when he saw the assembled employees. Onstage he introduced Conor as their new general manager, praised the way he'd cleaned up the club, outlined his history at Poor Richard's and Bar Ditto, and discussed the IPO (it was the first word of it for most; like God, Rex thought it best to withhold his plans). He led the applause and, while Conor was succinctly enunciating his philosophy as, "Get 'em in, get their money, get 'em out," ducked into the men's room.

The club's porter was named Koo. Usually Koo's first task of the evening was to mop up the men's room floor, because the yellow-crusted urinal dripped and the overnight accumulation put it under half an inch of water, but the staff meeting meant he hadn't yet started in on his duties. Staff knew about the puddle. Rex didn't. At the unthinkable sensation of something seeping into his Guccis he looked down, aghast.

"Conor!" he screamed. "Goddam fucking *shit!* GODDAM FUCKING *SHIT!*"

Conor ran in.

"What kind of a *dump* you running here? Sewage spilled in the bathrooms! *I RUINED MY GUCCIS!* Two-hundred-dollar shoes!"

Flicking his foot, he splattered his pants.

"Sorry, Rex."

Rex dabbed with paper towels. By a miracle there were some in the dispenser.

"Let's just call it the Leaky Urinal, roll it out, see who salutes? Dammit. *Dammit.* Get it fixed, your fucking *job* is on the line." Rex dragged his soggy feet across the showroom. "Hurry up, Perri. Two hundred fucking *dollars!*"

Perri followed, leaving with a flat, "Good meeting, guys."

Ginger bundled them into the limo with a slam of the door and they squealed up First Avenue.

Koo was apologizing when Conor interrupted.

"Koo, you get a raise," he said, and took the stage again. "Look, people, may be good, may be bad, for sure won't be easy. Any help you can give, much appreciated. Any problems, don't hesitate. OK, go get 'em. Lordy, do I need a drink," he added, and stepped off the platform.

Later that evening when Sly told him Perri was on the line, he took it downstairs.

"*Hey*-ya, Perri, what up?"

"*I'm* fine, Conor, it's Black who's seriously disturbed. Those were his favorite shoes. They'll never be the same again. Just wanted you to know."

"'Preciate it," said Conor.

He returned upstairs. Joey, half-crocked, was explaining to crowding comedians how he was one of the owners now. Conor pulled him to Ashley's table. She and Joey watched the show; Conor watched everything. For a moment towards the end of the evening he allowed himself some satisfaction at being there. Then he looked around and saw how much there was to be done. But this too gave him satisfaction.

Eventually the night was over and even his extended ordeal of closing out the register ended. Past 4:00 a.m., the last one out, he left carrying the night's receipts. Locking the door alertly, trying not to attract notice, he walked two blocks to the bank, dropped the bag in the night deposit and waited for a cab through several stoplight cycles.

Dawn was making the world vanishingly pallid. Conor had a sudden sense of New York's loneliness. Lights spilled red across the empty blacktop, and there were nervous clickings and hummings as though to say, "Well, if that didn't work — *green* light!"

And the lights spilled green.

14.

ONE AFTERNOON SHORTLY before Christmas Rosetta was working at her hobby while thinking about Topic A—her career. That Conor's ascendancy at the Gag Reflex brought her own break nearer, she was sure—she could feel Destiny at her back.

After deftly dropping the ending of *Arsenic and Old Lace*—the sweetly homicidal old ladies being removed to the madhouse—in place of *A Streetcar Named Desire*'s (Vivien Leigh, ditto), she put Vivien Leigh in place of Gloria Swanson being taken to the asylum in *Sunset Boulevard*.

She played back the edited endings, doubting anyone would notice a thing, much less get her mordant comment on American women's mid-20th-century status. But such is the fate of the artist.

Rewinding the videotapes, she got ready for another dreary weeknight going from one hole-in-the-wall to the next, for almost no money and considerable expense in taxis.

Dreary, but essential: Stand-up comedy is performance art. It requires polishing the material to a fare-thee-well, punching up the structure, razoring off every extraneous syllable, attacking at the right energy level and — *crucial* — doing it in front of audiences over and over again until it gets results guaranteed.

Rosetta had boiled her Poor Richard's show down to six minutes meant to kill on *Letterman* or — God willing — *Carson*. Kill on *Carson*, win Johnny's high-sign — thumb and forefinger held in a circle, the old *OK* — and a comedian was *set*: headliner status in clubs nationwide, sitcom guest appearances, even . . . *The Rosetta Stone Show*.

She patted her stuffed cat Smokey for luck, went down and flagged a cab.

"Smiles, please, Bond and Broadway."

Smiles was a dark and beery basement favored by NYU students. The harassed manager, short of bodies, told her she could go on right away, and the emcee introduced her.

"*Gnnnh . . . Gnnnh . . .*" she gnawed. "My, what a plump audience you are. *Mmm!* Bet you'd taste *delicious*." She explained her man-eating heritage. "But in New York I fit right in — your whole culture's cannibalistic. Funny how you know from its taboos what a society's *real* interests are, isn't it?"

Straight over their heads. No one laughed, except for a comedian in the rear (but Rosetta cherished her reputation as a comic's comic). She finished her routine, thumbed her stomach to produce her trademark belch, and went off.

"Tough crowd," said the bartender sympathetically.

"Really? Didn't notice. Maybe not as sharp as some."

A five-minute ride downtown to the Rictus, where the audience was hipper and drunker.

She felt she was going over.

"Used to call television the idiot box," she said, "but it's so much more the *id* box, don't you think? Expresses everything *we* don't dare to. We sit comatose watching murders, wars, love affairs, every kind of eruption. Why *do* anything when you can *watch* someone do it?" People chuckled uneasily. "Then again, as our supreme arbiter, it's also the *superego* box. Which I guess makes Freud the prophet of TV. But what can you say about a culture where even narcissism's becoming vicarious?"

A drunk started riding her.

"Hey, Poontang!" he called.

Handling hecklers is part of the game—collapse when drunks bully you and you're no pro. Rosetta was unfazed.

"So you want to tell us about your tiny little dick?" she asked. When his girlfriend protested, she riffed on "the *real* Heisenberg Effect: The way the same dick looks to different people. Look at what they say about Warhol's—friends call him big, enemies small. Or Charlie Chaplin's? Rep of the biggest in Hollywood, till Orson Welles called it a *peanut*. Like *yours*, sir."

Somehow the whole thing got out of hand. Rosetta could make people laugh, but she couldn't love them, wouldn't let them near. It was as if she carried the war on herself to a new battlefield with every stage she stepped on. But a performer has to love the audience while it's loving her for the circuit to be complete, for it to work.

The emcee lurched onstage.

"OK, that's enough. That's *enough*. Hear it for Rosetta Stone and her warped sense of humor! No? Rosetta, I was you—"

On to the next.

So Rosetta was warmed up when, around 10:30, she entered the Gag Reflex, just to look around, see what was doing, show herself. She'd only been there as a customer who found little to like in what was offered onstage, and had no reasonable expectation of being allowed to perform. But what are friends for?

Right off she smelled something rank: The sweat of high

stakes being exuded just where it was crucial to seem relaxed. She hung at the bar. Sly ignored her until Conor came by and said, "Buy her a drink."

"Conor, place looks great!"

"Thanks."

"So can I go on?"

"Set show tonight, Dolls."

"On a *Tuesday?*"

"Auditions."

"For who?"

"Claudia."

Claudia!

"Where's Ashley?"

"Inside."

"Can I?"

"Go ahead."

Rosetta pushed through the curtains and, blinking at the stage glare, dropped into a chair at an empty table. Perhaps 30 were in the room. Ashley sat with Claudia and party at the prime middle table, and Rosetta watched them watching.

Already Colin Quinn had killed, as had John Mendoza, Margaret Smith, Barry Steiger, Brett Butler, Larry David and Larry Miller.

Now Derf Talbuck was on. His act consisted of mocking his last few dates. Pretty old. He could get people going sometimes, though. She'd seen him get Hell Hole heaving with laughter. Scattered across the room a few were laughing now. But Claudia didn't laugh, not that her icy professional smile suffered.

Derf finished and Larry Amoros, emcee for the night, tried to restore a merry mood. Emcees have a hard job, but what was Letterman — Carson himself — if not an emcee? Rosetta had emceed women's nights at the Rictus, knew how to do it.

Larry brought on Tommy Hewitt.

Tommy's *shtick* was imitating his mother calling him in off the streets. He threw back his head and with his voice trailing off called: "Tom-*mee* . . . Tom-*mee* . . ."

A Dead End Kids thing, a generation late, if not two. Rosetta could only shake her head.

But Claudia laughed. Claudia laughed maniacally. So did her entourage.

Tommy redoubled his efforts: "Tom-*mee!* Tom-*mee!*"

Rosetta felt sick. Tommy would do Carson in three weeks, she *knew* it. Tommy was *made*. Had guest star written all over his face—unless, God forbid, "Tom-*mee!*" became a catchphrase that made him a star outright. (Why couldn't "*Gnnnh . . . Gnnnh . . .*" do it for *her?*)

Conor sat down next to her. She grabbed his crotch.

"Conor, I'm so hot tonight, I have to go on *right now*. I'll give you the best head you ever got if you let me walk up on that stage."

He laughed so hard Claudia looked over her shoulder. Rosetta could see Ashley, very bored.

"Make Ashley that offer and you may have a—"

"She go that way?"

"Nobody knows."

"I *will*," said Rosetta. "This *instant*."

She went over and whispered into Ashley's ear.

Ashley's head whipped backwards.

"No way," she said. "*Never*."

"Why not?"

"Because I say so, that's why. Bug off."

Rosetta went back to Conor's table.

"No go," she reported.

"Sucks," Conor said.

Next up was a watered-down Woody Allen—same face,

voice, whine; everything but the genius. Claudia sat up straight and commenced whispering to Ashley.

"I'm going to throw up," Rosetta said.

Claudia and party eventually left. The show went on, though the remaining performers were miffed at losing the one member of the audience who mattered. But Rosetta did see something interesting: Rex Black came in and sat at the table now empty but for Ashley. He leaned close, talking, and Ashley looked fixedly at the stage, while an odd refraction of the lights illumined something taking place beneath the table—his hand in hers, working, twisting, digging, gouging, pushing.

"See that?" she asked Conor.

"Whassat?"

"Conor, are you *drunk?*"

He shrugged. They sat for a while, and Rosetta went home.

15.

NEW YEAR'S EVE at the Gag Reflex was a brilliant success. Along with a champagne split, Conor gave every customer a pair of Groucho glasses (Frank's idea), and a New Year's tradition was born.

Business surged in the depths of winter. That stand-up comedy was hot—the subject of daily newspaper features and gossip items, plus weekly HBO specials—didn't hurt, but Conor's management had much to do with bringing in new customers. The place looked better day by day, new cheerfulness and efficiency prevailed among the staff. And the performers were happy when, at Conor's insistence, Rex jumped their stipends to $20 weeknights, $100 on weekends (it rocked the industry).

Conor was busy, absorbed and happy, all his formidable energies available to the club. He animatedly told Frank how Milton Berle, impossibly ancient, had been in to see a show, was persuaded to totter onstage, and blew the house away; how Rodney Dangerfield had reduced him and Ashley to going *"Boom!"* as every punchline landed; how for once Robin Williams (Conor's favorite, sweetest guy in the world) found the audience ice cold — stood up there, the sweat pouring off, unable to wring so much as a chuckle out of anybody.

More than ever, the club was a celebrity magnet, where Richie Havens and Edgar Winter could drop by to play impromptu sets to a warm welcome (Rex was in heaven), where Eddie Murphy or Warren Beatty and Julie Christie might catch a show.

Frank reminded Conor he wanted a job in Rex's office. Conor failed to pass on the idea to Joey or Perri, forgot to bring it up with Rex.

But Frank persisted. Conor's one complaint about his new job concerned how loath *the office* was to spend anything on improvements. For instance, the lack of a refrigerated beer box behind the bar meant that Koo had to keep hauling warm cases up from the cellar all evening, along with ice to cool them in the sinks (so long as the ancient ice machine held out). Rex thought the arrangement perfectly adequate. Frank argued that his being on the inside would help loosen the purse strings: Conor would get his beer box.

So on a late January morning Frank went for his job interview with Perri. He found the office and knocked on the door, without result. Downstairs the doorman told him no one was in yet. He waited. Perri soon hurried into the lobby and introduced herself.

"Sorry I'm late. Things are so hectic. Come on up." During the elevator ride she said, "Conor's great. I'm his biggest fan."

"Thank you."

As they stepped off they could hear the telephone ringing. Joey answered on tape, intoning poshly, "You have reached the headquarters of Gag Reflex, Incorporated, personal managers of tomorrow's comedy and music stars, and corporate parent of the Gag Reflex, New York's premier comedy club."

The tone sounded and Rex spoke as Perri unlocked the door and rushed inside.

"*Fuck!* Goddammit, Perri, it's past 10:00 in the morning, pick up! *Goddam fuck!*"

As she lifted the receiver he hung up.

"Excuse me a moment?" she asked, and left the room. Frank heard muffled retching.

The phone rang again and after Joey's recital Rex, subdued, said he was at the accountants'. He began heating up again: "I realize you're home on your knees worshipping the porcelain goddess of maternity, but can't you be sick at the office just as easy? *Fuck!*"

A door opened on a flushing toilet and Perri rushed in and picked up.

"Hello? Hello?" She hung up. "Too late!"

Frank helped her gather the mail spread over the floor. He liked her for coping cheerfully and, applying the algorithm which transforms a woman to her gay brother, found her attractive.

They sat down.

"Your résumé's impressive. Phi Beta Kappa? Master's? TIME Magazine? Why would you want to work *here?*"

He explained how his preparation to be an English professor ended in horror and disillusion when he taught his first courses as an adjunct, and how his subsequent disengagement from academia left him in some respects high and dry, if truer to himself. Also he mentioned his wish for something lively in the way of work.

"Show business is certainly lively."

"And it must be a goof dealing with celebrities."

She smiled a little uncertainly.

"But of course I also want to make Conor's life easier if I can."

"I can relate to that," she replied. "Do you type?"

"Sixty words a minute, and I know wordprocessing."

"Good, we might get a computer soon. Do you like comedy?"

"Love it."

"Music?"

"I have two of Tintinella's albums."

"She's no longer a client," Perri said. "Oh well, she's peaked anyway. We have a new superstar: *Racquel*. Well, Black certainly needs an assistant—someone to handle his crazy schedule—and I need an office manager."

"Sounds challenging."

She stood up.

"Let me talk it over with Black," she said. "I'll call you."

"Great."

As Frank was leaving Byrne trailed in, distracted and important in a white fur coat.

"Early audition," he told them. "But it looks good."

Perri called the next day and offered Frank the job at $350 a week. He was pleased. Conor said he was, too.

Although Conor suggested he stay on at TIME, at least until he saw how things worked out IPO-wise—and otherwise—to Frank's mind giving notice there was a token of commitment to his lover. So he did it.

He started the following Monday. He went in promptly, but had to wait by the elevator until Byrne showed. Byrne parked him on the sofa while he caught up on some personal calls.

Perri soon arrived, gave him a key and showed him what he was supposed to do.

"Let's see, if the phone rings and Byrne's busy, just answer it *Gag Reflex, Incorporated*. The *Incorporated* is important: Due diligence."

"Where should I sit?"

"Um, take Ashley's desk for now." She gestured at the only free desk. "Do you know her? Books the club?"

"No." Frank had been avoiding the club so as not to complicate Conor's life.

"She's very nice."

While Frank sorted the mail, Perri studied an album of club snapshots.

The telephone rang. Byrne's sidelong glance indicated that he couldn't get off his call, so Frank answered and crisply informed a woman: "One continuous show beginning at 8:30, with a cover charge of $5 per person and a two-drink minimum . . . Depends on who comes by, Dennis Miller and Richard Lewis were in last night . . . Can't take your reservation here, but if you call the club after 4:00 o'clock . . ."

"Good, you know the spiel," said Perri.

The phone rang again. It was Rex, welcoming him aboard. Hanging up, Frank said, "To quote Mr. Black, 'ETA five minutes.'"

The door swung open and Joey was halfway across the room before he saw Frank and put on the brakes.

"Hey, hot stuff! You one of us?"

"Hey, Joey! Guess I am."

"Cool!" Joey embraced him, then revolved and spread out a brochure in front of Perri. "Perri, look at this. Stopped at the Arcades East to look at condos."

"Are they nice?

"*Gorgeous!* Dig the two-bedroom: three baths and a *terrace!*"

"Pretty! What's it go for?"

"Four-fifty."

"Pricey?"

"Investment, after the IPO," Joey explained. "Should see it, lobby's like a London club. Doormen dress up like fucking

Beefeaters. Salesman says price is going up to half a million soon."

"Wouldn't be surprised."

They studied floorplans until Joey asked, "Perri, could I hit up petty cash for $20 till payday?"

"If we have it," she answered. Taking out a cigar box, she found a bill inside and handed it to him.

"Thanks," he said. "Hear about Dimitri Donner?"

"The Mets outfielder? Was *he* in last night?"

"Yeah—"

"Frank, could you find me Cindy Adams at the *Post?* She's in the Rolodex."

"Um, Dimitri got smashed," Joey said. "And when Hank went on, he started heckling."

"What did he say?"

"Um, *Jewboy* was about the best of it."

"How was Hank?"

"It got to him, would anybody. Upset."

"Oh," said Perri.

"Conor went over to talk to Dimitri, who's huge," said Joey. "So I went over, too? And Adrian from the door, and Helga— What's that big waitress's name?"

"Lola?"

"Well, no one laid a hand on, he went, but noisy. We had to hold Hank back. Would have got killed."

Frank reached Cindy Adams' card to Perri, but she sorrowfully refused it. Arm still extended, he said, "You could just mention Dimitri Donner enjoyed the show."

"That's a thought."

Perri took the card and made the call (the item appeared that afternoon).

"This is so cool, Frank," Joey repeated. "Conor will be so happy."

"And maybe I'll get to see him sometimes, in between the celebs."

Laughing, Joey vanished into his cubbyhole.

Someone knocked at the door. Frank opened it to find a notably nondescript person regarding him.

"Morning, Mr. Rex Black in?"

"No," Frank said, and instinctively lied: "He's on the Coast."

Joey looked over, astonished.

"Out of town and you don't expect him, huh?"

"That's right."

"Well, tell Mr. Rex Black to consider himself served," said the man, flipping papers into the room.

Frank closed the door and picked them up. The door opened again and Rex entered, a manila envelope tucked under his arm.

"Fuck!" he said. "Who was that jerkoff?" He grabbed the papers. "Process server! Can always spot 'em!"

"What is it, Black?"

"Shit, that scumbag Marvin's *suing* me?" said Rex. "Fucking *believe* it? Over *T-shirts?*"

"It's a lot of T-shirts."

"Wait for the IPO, he's got the national concession! The whole fucking chain! Stack that against this measly 17 thou!"

"Black," said Perri, "this is—"

"The boyfriend, eh? I remember." Rex handed him the manila envelope. "Take this."

"Sure."

"Don't let me see it again or—more important—the auditors or the SEC."

"No problem."

Frank put it in a desk drawer.

"What's in it, Black?" asked Perri.

Rex looked at her for a moment.

"Guest checks from the club."

"Don't the auditors need them?"

"Only *think* they do. Don't have these, that lowers the gross, which raises the margin, makes the club look like a gold mine—and *that* helps the IPO. Siggy's idea." He turned to Frank. "The auditors want a look around the club, so call Conor, tell him to go let 'em in, give 'em the run of the place—anything they want."

"He's sleeping."

"Fuck, I *know* he's sleeping," said Rex, "but the auditors want in. Tell Sir Conor to hotfoot it up there."

Conor had it by the third ring. Frank could see him flying down from the loft bed, expecting to hear about a fouled-up liquor delivery or a waitress with cramps.

"Hello?" came his croak.

"Hey, honey."

"Shit, Dolls, trying to get some Z's here."

"I'm sorry, but Mr. Black wants you to let some auditors into the club."

"When?"

"Right away."

"*Fuck!* Frank, I did not get you that job so you could wake me up!"

"I don't like it either, Conor."

"Don't make me sorry. I'll be at the club in an hour."

Frank hung up and reported.

"He OK?" asked Rex.

"He's not an early riser."

Rex asked Perri, "What are you working on?"

"Looking for pictures that would look good in the prospectus."

"*I'll* tell you what would look good," said Rex. "Steve

95

Martin. Gabe Kaplan."

"Remember what Harshaw said about the permission issues? They could sue."

"Thought that over. Know what I came up with?"

"What?"

"*Fuck* them! The Gag Reflex gave 'em spots when they were starting out."

"What if they see the prospectus?"

"*If?* Bet your *ass* they'll see it! And they'll think, 'Weren't those the days?' — *and* buy shares." He rapped one photo. "Martin with the arrow through his head? *Classic!* Joey!"

"*Yo!*"

Joey scrambled around the corner.

"What you working on?"

"The Come-Ons' new look. My hair-cutter says — "

"Ice it. Racquel called last night, played me a new demo, piece of shit anthem: *The End of Time*. Talk to her. Work on it. Jazz it up."

"Got it."

Racquel was recording her crucial first album with Janos — L.A.'s hottest producer — for whose services Rex, more optimistic than her label, was paying.

He went into his office and got on the phone.

"Frank, important!" Perri said. "When one of the clients calls for Black, put them through. If he's on another call, make sure he knows they're waiting."

"The Golden Rule of personal managers," sniffed Byrne.

"Do you have a client list?" Frank asked.

Perri counted on her fingers.

"It's Racquel, The Come-Ons, Hank Washburn." She looked embarrassed. "We're in negotiations with more."

Savage eruptions from Rex's office ended in his slamming down his phone and striding into the bullpen.

"Fucking *turd*! It *kills* me, we're catching the wave, on the *verge*, and Marvin's bleating about *T-shirts*? '*Marvin*' — I tell him — 'wait six months, I'll open Gag Reflexes in Toronto and Vegas and L.A., you'll be selling coast-to-coast. *Marvin*' — I tell him — 'I'm going to make you *rich!*' 'Gimme my money now,' he says. Stupid *schmuck*! Just for spite, Perri, take him off the list. He's the last one we pay — the *last!*"

"OK, Black, but we need T-shirts. Conor says the mediums are almost out."

"*Fuck!* All I ask is a little belief! Aren't I entitled to a little *belief*? A little *cooperation*? A little goddam fucking *loyalty*?"

He slammed the glass door shut. Always in closing it he assumed for a moment the attitude of Christ crucified. Perri went back to her pictures. Joey clamped on headphones. Byrne cautiously resumed murmuring into the phone.

At 3:00 o'clock, shortly after Byrne ran out to an audition, Ashley entered the office. She stopped short, horrified eyes on Frank.

"Am I fired?" she asked.

"Do I have your desk? Let me move. I'm Frank."

"Oh, are you?"

Joey leapt between them.

"Frank, this is Ashley Parrish — booker to the stars."

"Pleased to meet you."

"I'm sure."

Frank moved to Byrne's desk.

"Not there," Perri cautioned. "He might be back."

He saw no other available desk. Neither did Perri.

"Just for today, then," she said.

The day wore away in red-alert crises. Frank liked it. Everything and everyone was novel to him, but he enjoyed sorting things out, trying to be effective on the phone and on paper. He felt like a many-armed deity — assistant deity —

sitting in the lotus position, achieving serenity through maximum activity.

As his arms multiplied, he was thinking, "I'm *in!* I'm *in!*"

16.

FROM THE START FRANK rejoiced in the way his job fused with his relationship. When he murmured goodbye to his lover in the morning, Conor's long lashes fluttered and his body seized like a cat's hearing endearments, and Frank felt equipped for another day of fighting on his behalf.

Events surprised them at every turn in Rex's office—it ran strictly according to the crisis of the day—but Frank felt gratifyingly stimulated, absorbed and useful. What he liked best, sitting at his new desk next to Perri's, was pulling abreast of some longstanding problem and solving it; he usually found himself free to try, so long as it didn't involve spending anything (though he was balked in his scheme of firing Byrne when Perri stated unanswerably, "But he's so good-looking!").

One project he pursued after taking his first paycheck to the bank and having it thrown back in his face. "Cash it at the club next weekend," Perri told him. "Everybody does."

So it proved: The Gag Reflex routinely issued paychecks with nothing in the bank to cover them, instead cashing them out of the club's fat weekend grosses.

"What's the big deal?" Conor wondered.

"Besides being *stupid*, it's not right," Frank fumed. "And

it's not going to happen again."

Studying the existing procedure, he found that the payroll account had last dibs on the club's receipts. He changed this to give it *first* call by directing Conor to deposit the receipts not into the corporate account — as heretofore — but into the operating account, from which he could wire sufficient over to payroll first thing Monday (payday) morning.

The wire transfers carried Rex's signature, expertly forged by Joey if Rex was unavailable. ("Hey, that's how my ride here started," Joey assured Frank. "Needed somebody to autograph Tintinella's glossies for the fans.")

Simple, but for the first time banks would honor a Gag Reflex paycheck.

Another idea was to put in a pay phone at the club. Supervising its installation one afternoon of spitting snow, Frank wandered through the showroom while the technician worked out front.

The showroom surprised him. Recently things had gone missing from Conor's apartment, to the extent that it was taking on a dismantled air. One day Frank asked where the plaster nude flourishing a red lightbulb — prize of a Carmine Street trash can — had gotten to. Conor stared at the empty space, then remembered: "Oh, it's up at the club. Looks *great.*"

And there it was, among the *tchotchkes* on the shelves Conor built onstage. Half his collection, it seemed, was there or arrayed around the walls. He was delighted whenever a performer riffed on an object, ecstatic when it happened during a TV taping. The most popular was an old wind-up wall phone comedians took to using to improv themselves out of trouble.

To Frank it was a peculiar fraying of the texture of the life he shared with Conor.

Meanwhile the phone behind the bar rang from time to

time and, answering it, he took several reservations. Shortly after 4:00 o'clock, Mary the phone person showed up and took over.

It gave him an idea he brought up at the next meeting.

"About reservations," he said. "Mary goes in at 4:00 –"

"Sometimes," said Perri, whose temper was suffering as her belly swelled. "She's late a lot."

"But the phone rings all day long. No one answers if they call before she gets there. What if – instead of calling back later – they call the Comic Strip or The Improv? We're giving away business."

Rex snapped forward.

"Way they did it from the start, Germano *never* had a phone person in before 4:00."

"But he didn't have a separate office. We could put Call Forwarding on the club's reservations line and forward it here last thing at night. During the day *we* take the reservations, then when Mary comes in, she un-forwards the line and we dictate our names to her."

Rex frowned. "That's a good idea. Perri, isn't that a good idea?"

"Yeah, Black, but why haven't we done it before now?"

"I'll tell you why: 'Cause everyone else working for me's a *dick,* that's why!"

Joey laughed so hard he almost fell out of his chair.

"Should try it out on Conor," said Ashley.

"Tell him, Frank, OK? But call the phone company right now."

That night Conor came home angry.

"*Shittiest* idea I ever heard," he told Frank. "Didn't expect it from *you.*"

"Letting customers make reservations when they want? I don't see –"

"They want a reservation, they call after *4:00.*"

"But if they don't, we end up with empty seats. Why make it harder for anyone who goes to the trouble of calling in the first place?"

"Shit, that's *heat.* Hell, we were smart, we'd get an unlisted number, lose the sign! That's what people *want,* to feel special they even heard of you."

"Forwarding the line's no big deal — is it? Thirty seconds?"

"You don't *get* it, do you, Frank? *I'm* general manager. That club's *my* responsibility. If Rex doesn't like the way I do things, he can fire me.

"You're supposed to have my back? This feels like a *stab.*"

"Conor!"

"May not mean to, Dolls, but you're undermining me. What hurts is you never gave me a chance to knock it down. Oh, no, *I* hear about it when it's a done deal, because *you* went behind my back."

"Conor, you're right, I should have talked with you first," said Frank. "But I still think it's the right business decision."

"You just don't *get* it," Conor repeated.

"Sorry, Conor, I really am."

In bed Conor gave him his back. It was a wall without handholds. And though Frank wasn't sure of it for a few days, given the mismatch in their hours, he stopped speaking to him, too.

The new system netted a half dozen additional covers every weeknight. These vindicated the business decision, but didn't alleviate the misery of their estrangement.

A few nights later, Frank said, "Conor, it's ludicrous to let anything from the job come between us."

"Right as always, Dolls," Conor broke his embargo to say. "*Ludicrous.*"

Next day Frank got home from work to find the living

room arranged like a crime scene. Conor's TV-watching quilt lay crushed on the La-Z-Boy. Poking out from a fold was a bottle of Jergens lotion. A box of Kleenex lay on the floor, and several crumpled tissues were glued to the rug beside the latest *Blueboy*. A porn tape sat in the VCR.

He left everything as he found it. He was hurt, not that Conor was masturbating — it was his own unhappy outlet, after all — or even using pornography, but that he would make a show of it, a show of depriving him.

When at dawn Conor brought the quilt upstairs, Frank sat up and asked, "Can we talk?"

Conor's face clenched.

"It's important."

"Shoot."

"When I got home from work, it was obvious you'd been jerking off to a porn tape —"

"Shit, *now* what?" said Conor. "Let me run to Confession! Yeah, I admit it. *Mea culpa*. But you jerk off, too, let me guess."

"Sure —"

"Don't hear *me* complain."

"What bothers me is you left it so I'd see —"

"That's right, *you're* the soul of discretion. Every soiled Kleenex flushed. To the manner born."

"Can't we talk about these things?"

"Sex was never the biggest thing with us," Conor remarked, accurately enough.

"But I love you, and want to express that sexually, and —"

"Noted," said Conor. "By the way, ever need porn, ask Sly: *Amazing* collection."

He reestablished his embargo, to the extent that Frank's "Good night" brought forth not even a grunt.

Tired of having *Mute* pressed in his direction, the next day Frank took his razor and toothbrush back to his own place.

Conor didn't say a word.

Conor never confided his innermost secrets, but he used to shout them out sometimes at the Dick after last call, when the gate came crashing down on staff and a few favored regulars for a last raucous hour, a screamfest where *everything* came out. It was from his occasional attendance that Frank had learned what he knew about his lover.

Conor was born and raised in Elmhurst, Queens. His father was a machinist, his mother a housewife, and both the children of Irish immigrants. Like his seven brothers and sisters he attended Catholic school, but Conor was the brightest of the bunch, and where the others went on to public high school, he won a scholarship to a Jesuit day school.

There was money at Ignatius Prep, and money made the distinctions it always does, but in a Jesuit school athletics or brains can trump money, and so can good looks.

Glances followed Conor from boyhood. He was an altar boy, and old Father Murray once (if only once) was heard to attribute half the attendance at 6:30 a.m. Mass to lust for the angel positioning the salver beside him (Father Murray didn't do justice to his own fame for saying an 18-minute Mass). Father Shaefer soon grabbed him for his choir (the events that saw him sentenced to 30 years still lay in the future).

At 14, when most boys' bodies are going wrong, Conor grew into a supremely comfortable physical fit with himself. His body graduated every motion gracefully, gave every step an insinuation; he inspired instant interest in girls and boys, women and men. Playing Frederic in *The Pirates of Penzance*, a co-production with the neighboring girls school, when he bestrode the stage in tights he had merely to present his lordly little backside for the young ladies of St. Mary's to feel blindly for each other's hands and vent moans of desire.

Coach liked to watch Conor undress, which he did with the

sensuality of Michelangelo's *Dying Slave*, smiling and aware (on some unconscious level) as he pulled up his shirt and pushed down his pants. Coach showered with his boys, lazily polishing his testicles while they, hairless fledglings, perched as briefly as possible beneath the spray; except for Conor, who stood dynamically modeling himself while the water pouring over his body made it gleam like marble.

This was animal blessedness on his part. But even with older brothers in the house, Conor had no idea what masturbation was until Father Brady showed him.

Father Brady taught Latin at Ignatius. Ninth-grade boys were so disoriented — new to high school, new to their own bodies and voices — that if he set his class each in turn to translate out loud a sentence of Julius Caesar's treatise on Gaul, Father Brady could preside standing over Conor's desk, an attentive frown on his face and Latin corrections coming out of his mouth while his forefinger stroked Conor's silken nipple to crispness.

Conor's was not the only shirt Father Brady delved into, but no one said anything, no one *ever*. Ninth graders were perfectly safe. No one would even remember; self-respect lowered the mantle of amnesia. After 20 years at Ignatius, Father Brady knew this for certain. In the *10th* grade Conor wouldn't have endured it; 10th-grade boys *won't*. But in the 9th grade it was delicious and safe for Father Brady to dip his hand into Conor's shirt, thumb down the yoke of his undershirt and feel his warm muscled breast, while keeping a weather eye out for whatever might happen in his lap.

Conor would sit there, face violently red. When his turn came he'd make a hash of it.

"*Puellarum* is genitive," Father Brady might gently remind him, before prompting the next boy: "Mr. Cassidy?"

One day he summoned Conor to the 3rd-floor Residence to

discuss an extra-credit project. Setting him up on his sofa with cookies and Coke, the priest adjourned through two open doors to take a shower. Reappearing in a robe, he sat down and quoted Virgil while his hand stole up Conor's thigh.

An hour later he sent Conor off late to basketball practice with the excuse of having started a special tutorial. Coach laughed out loud. Father Brady meanwhile repaired next door and asked Father O'Brien to hear his Confession.

The following August Conor "broke your mother's heart" (in his father's piquant phrase) by announcing that he would attend 10th grade at public Newtown High. He refused pointblank to return to Ignatius, not that he could give any adequate reason for so self-destructive a course. He did offer one, but it sounded lame even to himself: "I'm 15 now."

He spent three years at Newtown, meeting in his first week there the girl he would fuck every afternoon until, at dawn following senior prom, he dropped her in the surf at Jones Beach. He won a scholarship to NYU (earning a degree in theatrical set design), moved to Greenwich Village, began going with *men,* told more people than cared to hear of it that he was *gay,* and at the height of its fame got a job as a bare-chested busboy at Studio 54. He quit when he learned he was expected to blow customers in a certain basement room, and went to work instead for the caterer Donald Bruce White. Soon he added a second job bartending at Bar Ditto.

Many desired Conor, but in the main he bestowed himself on guys he happened across in his moments of need. No one who had him had any reason to complain – he was *hot,* even if animal blessedness seldom accompanied him to bed, where he was surprisingly brusque and averse to kissing.

Nor despite strong scenes at home did Conor after entering Newtown High attend Mass or in any way operate as a Catholic. He was repelled by a theology so powerful it can explain everything under heaven except gay people. "I'm an atheist," he liked to say, "and I've got the Catholic schooling to prove it."

The upshot was that Conor regarded his sexuality not as an expression of his most personal self, but as a thing of whim. So, too, whether he went with women or men: *whim*. Moreover, sex only meant relief from immediate physical pressure; it was incapable of contributing to emotional connection. To make sex a constructive element of something lasting touched areas of himself so vulnerable and painful they were walled off for good.

For whatever its origins, pain filled every cavity of Conor's being. Drinking dyed it, crystallized it, set it apart, made it bearable. Naturally he made the bar business his profession, dwelt where buzz drowns out every clamor and another flippant round dissolves any pain.

Frank might have gone ahead and played around, reasoning it would deprive Conor of nothing while reducing to himself the cost of maintaining his commitment. But commitment has its price, and he was willing to pay it, even if it meant starving for sex. Not to, after all, would prove the relationship it supported to be illusory.

He did come to two conclusions. The first was that, in being attracted to Conor's depth of feeling, in effect he loved him *for* his pain. That seemed screwed up. The second was that probably what Conor saw in *him* was somebody so involved with his own inner life that he sensed a relationship with him would cost less of himself than one with someone more extroverted. That was, if not screwed up, distinctly unflattering.

For the first time, he realized there were problems in the relationship.

Perri asked what was wrong.

"Conor's not speaking to me," Frank admitted.

"Guys have a fight?"

"Not really. We disagree about forwarding the phones, that's all. Seems I stepped on his turf. We'll work it out."

17.

FEBRUARY, THAT HAG IN RAGS, finally inched her noisome self off the scene and gave way to March — except, it seemed, in Rex's office, which late one afternoon was suffering from wintry *mal-de-due-diligence*. Ashley was over the top at her roommate's antics, Perri's morning sickness knew no clock, suppliers yelled at Frank for their money, Joey's band demanded action and Byrne was threatening to abandon show business altogether.

After taking a call from the producer of Racquel's album, Rex summoned Joey to his office and slid the door shut.

"Janos just called," he said. "What's this about *friction* in the *studio?*"

Joey almost fled to his cubbyhole.

"The second track?"

"*Yeah,* second track."

"Shouldn't get political," Joey said. "They finished *The End of Time* and Janos is in love with it. Second track and first single, he thinks."

"*You* like it?"

"For my *funeral,* sure," Joey assured him. "Fine for the

single's B side, Rex, but album's second track is for her most important statement."

"Which is?"

"*Put Your Heat in Me*. Great first single, too."

"Piece of shit *dance* song?"

"*Great* hook, could go Number One," Joey said. "And you know my theory about personal pronouns –"

"Settled, Joey," Rex told him. "What Janos wants, Janos gets. But what the *fuck* is Racquel doing laying down anything *not* Number One material?"

"There're going to be ten songs on that album –"

"Your *ass* is on the line."

"Rex, she turns 30 next month," Joey said steadily. "This is her last shot. She'll deliver."

"Friction in the fucking *studio!*"

"What it really is," said Joey, and stopped.

"*Yeah?*"

"I don't know. Funny chemistry there."

"Thought he was such a cocksman?"

"She's hot for her boyfriend."

"*Shit!*"

Joey returned to his cubbyhole and was grooving to headphones before Rex finished his survey of Carnegie Hall.

"Joey!" yelled Rex.

Ashley and Frank failing to get Joey's attention, Rex marched out and yanked off the headphones himself.

"Joey, *goddam fuck!*"

"*Yo.*" Joey leapt up.

"*Put Your Heat in Me* as first single?"

"Uptempo, Latin, dirty: *Yeah!* Can't miss!"

"For the video?"

"I see pedalpushers, convertibles, some guy with his shirt off."

"You would," said Rex. "Janos wants *The End of Time* and his guy Clark directing."

"Shit."

"Problem?"

"That means Racquel wringing her hands against a brick wall with her skirt hiked up."

"Hiked to kingdom come! And no underwear: We're gunning for Madonna Butterfly here!"

"Cliché," said Joey.

"I am *surrounded* by assholes," said Rex, crossing to his office and bouncing the door shut as he reenacted Calvary. *"Surrounded!"*

He jerked it open again.

"Joey, this fucking album's *key*. It's going to say in the prospectus that we have a hot new singer with a record Janos *himself* produced and if, when they read that, it's not climbing the charts— And while *I* pay the freight, they're *bickering?"*

"Rex—"

"Take care of it, Joey."

Slam!

Joey got on the phone to the Coast.

It amused Perri to see Ashley burning the candles and rearranging the crystal pyramids that now bored her. Having left macrobiotics behind, she devoted herself to a single new interest: eating. Not six months gone, she was tremendous, her arms finned by wattles of flesh, mighty at the hips.

"Came home last night, and there was Dickhead," Ashley was telling her. "My roommate's boyfriend? And she was raving drunk, as usual. I had it out with both of them. I can't take any more."

"About time," said Perri, squashing a foil blossom of chocolate to her lips. *"And—?"*

"He's getting a divorce."

Perri shook her head.

"No, he *told* me," Ashley insisted.

"Once a *schmuck*, always a *schmuck*," Perri said. "She can't win with Dickhead: If he leaves the wife, he's the kind who does that, and she'd be a fool to think he's there for *her*. Stays with her, your roommate gets *zilch*. Runs a company, you say? Wife's set, then."

"Perri, it's not all about *getting*. Stupid cow has no idea what's going on."

"Pregnant? More on her mind just now," Perri said. "I speak from experience. Want this?"

She held out her daughter's latest sonogram. Ashley flinched, then, relenting, propped it on her desk and, sighing, answered her phone. Perri returned to ageing the bills and conferring with Frank about which vendors to risk stiffing.

Rosetta Stone chose that discouraging afternoon to bring by her newest 8x10. It showed her smiling open-mouthed, incisors sharpened by an airbrush, little bones spelling out *Rosetta Stone the Man-Eater*.

The elevator trundled her upstairs and left her in the hallway. No one was around. She couldn't resist. Kneeling at the door, she thumbed open the mail slot.

Revealed to her was the Gag Reflex office as it was when only insiders were there, gleaming through the aperture with Cinemascope glamour. She wanted desperately to be a client, to have them hop about serving *her* interests, yak on the phone finding *her* gigs, shovel a little fame and fortune *her* way.

Although no one appeared to be hopping about for any reason whatsoever. Rex cast angry glances into the bullpen. Perri shuffled paper. Ashley blew smoke at what looked like a little Quattrocento Madonna, while occasionally addressing low remarks into the phone. From Frank and Byrne and Joey came desultory phone conversation.

The sight of Joey fascinated Rosetta. Never was he without a self-conscious rock-and-roll sizzle, but there he was offstage, backed up to his desk out of everyone's sight, one arm bunching and lifting his long hair as he talked on the phone. A few sharp words traveled to her: ". . . Yeah, but Rex *knows* you can't put a crappy *dance* song in the second slot."

As he listened to the response he arched his back, stretched his legs, clenched his face. Then peace reigned. Had he farted? Rosetta's guess was confirmed in the most surprising way when he shoved his hand down the back of his pants and, moving the phone aside for a second, passed his cupped palm beneath his nose.

She'd never seen anything like it. Her instinctive signalization of the moment—rattling the mail slot—was probably proof of genius. Joey jumped, and Perri looked sharply over. Rosetta stood up and opened the door so smoothly the rattle seemed, in retrospect, part of that act.

"Hullo, everybody."

"Rosie, were you watching through the mail slot?"

"Hullo, Perri. What do you mean?"

She knew her face had been invisible.

"Nothing."

"Why?" asked Rosetta. "Someone doing something they shouldn't? Jerking off in there, Joey? No, brought my new headshot. Best yet."

She saw that Ashley's Madonna in fact was a sonogram showing a fetus's head devoutly folded.

Joey brought her into his cubbyhole, exclaimed over her headshot, then made another call while she sat forgotten. Byrne remembered a late audition. Frank gave up and went home. Perri and Ashley prepared to leave for the day.

"Don't forget to lock up, Black or Joey," Perri called as Ashley helped her maneuver out the door.

"Think Rex will like my picture?" Rosetta asked Joey.

"Go on in and show him," he said. "I've got to split."

So Joey was waving from the door when Rosetta tapped at the glass and startled Rex, who was barking over the telephone.

He waved her into a seat while, legs crossed, one foot doing the work of a Tommy gun, he railed across the wire. "Yeah, putting 20 more chairs in the room . . . How? Hell, *I* don't know. My manager told me no can do, I said, 'Like your *job?* Look at the Bottom Line, Village Gate: fucking *cattle* cars. I want it so tight if one asshole gets up to pee, whole *table's* got to.'"

He finally hung up and Rosetta showed him her glossy.

"Hey, great picture! What's it mean, *Man-Eater?*"

"Means I'm very oral," she said. "Told Conor I'd blow him if he put me on your stage, and I wasn't kidding."

"He wouldn't be interested."

"No. So I told Ashley I'd eat her out."

"Did, huh?" His foot came down widely separated from the other.

"A five-minute shot, Rex, that's all I want, and I'll go with whatever the room decides. If I don't *kill* in five minutes, I'll never bother you again."

Rex looked at her. He stopped breathing. She watched his hand steal towards his crotch, and went, "*Gnnnh . . . Gnnnh . . .*"

He lunged for the miniblinds and lowered them against the lights beginning to spangle up to the sky. They heard the elevator laboring.

"Door locked?" he asked.

"Yes," she guessed.

He sat down again. Realizing she was missing her cue, she came around and fell on her knees.

"Hey, I don't *do* this," Rex protested.

"Didn't think you *did*," Rosetta responded. "Neither do *I*."

He reached into her waistband and pulled up her shirt. Her breasts bobbed free and he dove for them. Then he lay back, lifting his shirttails and pulling open his pants.

"If you want a sneak preview," he said.

She gobbled the fine-grained, red-hot flesh he presented. After a minute he stood up, placing his hands on her head and imposing a more deliberate pace. Her mouth flailed, gasped, found its rhythm. He probed and plowed it mercilessly, plugging her throat. She gagged, but—her face in the middle of a bad dream—suppressed the reflex.

"*Yeah!*" went Rex as he yielded, clamping her head tight. "*Yeah!*"

His breathing eased and his hold loosened. She released him. He found tissues and she spat into one.

As he tucked in his shirt, he asked brightly, "What was *that* all about?"

Coughing, she beat her chest and gasped, "I'm fine." She plucked a hair from her teeth, or pretended to.

"Bathroom's in there," he said.

She went in. Water ran.

"Got to get going," he called. She came out. "Look, tell me what day you want to go on, I'll tell Ashley."

"Thursday, 10:00 o'clock."

"You got it."

She left.

"One word to anybody," Rex yelled after her, "and you're out of the industry!"

18.

REX HAD FORGOTTEN he was hosting Siggy Brewster at the club that Thursday.

Siggy debouched from the Daimler with a party of prospective investors and a leggy blonde.

"Mandy was so looking forward, but something came up. This is Shanna."

His heavy hitters were dour types who drank rapidly and watched the stage through slitted eyes. Rex hoped that in the evening's latter stages, when the liquor was beginning to tell and the jokes getting raunchy, they'd tilt their chairs back and laugh louder than they'd laughed in public since high school, look around indulgently and right their chairs convinced that if comedy was the rock and roll of the Eighties, they were at Zeitgeist Central.

Hank Washburn performed soon after Siggy and his guests arrived. Unfortunately, he bombed.

Hank was Rex's personal discovery, a comedian who, having worked doggedly all over town for years, one night struck him as so *ready* that he signed him to a management contract the next day.

Ashley couldn't get Hank on *Letterman*, but did succeed in booking him on Joy Behar's short-lived first talk show. At the taping Rex sat in the front row, poised to laugh riotously.

From the control room the director spotted his fixed grin and wheeled in a camera to get the guffaws it promised. A gaffer paid out cable as silent hydraulics lofted the lens. Its operator brought its barrel boring in on Rex while, with heavy tread, Hank's first punchline approached.

It arrived, the camera's eye burned red and Rex's brain commanded, "Laugh! *Laugh!*" Instead his dry lips separated unevenly. In close-up. On national TV. (His only saving thought was, *Lifetime Network*.)

Those were his first misgivings concerning Hank. Now, sitting next to Siggy, the thought bubbled up, "Hank's not funny. Hank *Washburn*? Hank *Washed-Up*." But he managed to shove it into unconsciousness and give Hank the high-sign as the band played him off the stage. (To Sly, Hank complained that one whole side of the room lacked native English speakers.)

Rick the emcee cracked some jokes and, as the band launched into *Man-Eater*, announced, "At the Gag Reflex for the first time, here's the Man-Eater herself, Miss *Rosetta Stone*."

Rex touched Siggy's sleeve. "Cutting edge," he whispered. Siggy passed the word to his guests.

Conor, curious to see how Rosetta might go over, came in and sat beside Ashley.

Rosetta walked onstage and gnawed at the mic.

"*Gnnnh . . . Gnnnh . . .* Thank you," she said. "Thank you very much. Do appreciate it. Especially because of what it took to get me up here at long last. Ten years in the business, but this is my first appearance at the Gag Reflex. Know why? Know what I had to do to get on this stage? I had to blow the owner! Just to get this spot! Actually had to take his nasty in my mouth! (Not saying I *swallowed,* though.) Is he here? Rex Black, are you out there? Rex? Rex?"

Shading her eyes, she searched the audience, pretending not to see Rex until enough hands eagerly rayed towards him that he was compelled to half stand and wave. The audience loved it. Siggy was laughing so hard he spat up his drink.

"Thanks again, Rex. Don't think I'm complaining, it was only a small inconvenience. (Know what comes in little packages? Little things.) And a brief one.

"That's the audition process here: 'Open wide.' But Rex is going public soon, and I'm a little worried. Yes, this very club will soon have stockholders — *thousands* of them! Not sure my knees can hold out. Not to mention my *throat.*"

Siggy was choking. Rex clapped him on the back and shot Ashley a horrified stage whisper: "Get her off! I never want this fucking *lying* bitch on my stage again!"

Ashley hit a toggle switch and opposite the stage a light Rosetta alone could see flashed red. This red light meant, *Wrap it up and get off!*

She ignored it.

"But that's the American way. We're climbing that ladder of success, every one of us. Do whatever it takes to get to the next rung. Which usually involves getting fucked one way or another, doesn't it? You know what I mean. (Yes, I can tell you do.) But if someone puts it up you, at least you won't fall off your rung: It's rung security.

"The other way to hang on is by sticking your nose in the brown part of the next one up. But you have to be careful, 'cause there's no cosmetic solution. Surprising, when you think about it, but Estée Lauder completely overlooks the market — which in New York *alone!* Think of it! *Maquillage de couverture de brun nez.* Sounds great in French, *n'est pas?* 'Brown-nose pancake.' But then, wherever you have people, you'll find assholes, and you can quote me on that: Rosetta's Law."

Siggy, heaving with laughter, clung to Shanna for balance.

Toggle toggle toggle; the red light strobed.

"Look at *this* guy," Rosetta continued, singling out Siggy. "Built like a gorilla. So how come the blonde has her ass screwed into his lap? Could it be—a rung on her ladder of success? In other words, *money?* I think it's a possibility."

Siggy roared. Ashley made the international throat-cutting sign at Rick, who marched onstage applauding and grabbed the mic out of Rosetta's hands.

"Give it up for Rosetta Stone the Man-Eater!" he genially commanded.

Rosetta accepted her ovation. She dispensed little bows with palms pressed together, then opened her arms to the audience, radiating love, and applauded *it.* Triumph! Success! *Breakthrough!*

Face shining, she swept into the front bar. Behind her, Rick remarked, "Rosetta Stone, the one and only. One and only appearance *here,* I'm betting."

"*Terrific,* Rex," said Siggy, wiping his face. "Got a winner there."

"*Sensational,*" Siggy's guests told Rex. "Tells it like it *is.*"

"What's the commotion?" Sly asked as Rosetta took a stool and ordered Scotch.

"They love me!" she told him. "A star is born!"

"You *passed?*" he asked in surprise.

"Listen for yourself," she said happily. He gave her the drink—comedians who passed their auditions drank free forevermore—and she was touching glasses with other comics when Rex stalked past with Ashley.

"Rex, told you I'd go with whatever the room decided, and they loved me! I *killed.*"

"That right? From where I sat you *sucked*."

"No, that was the other day."

"Cut her off, Sly. Rosetta, I want you *out* of my club. She's 86'd, Conor. Come on, Ash."

They left without waiting to see how she took his decree, which was by making that Scotch *last* while she regaled Conor, Sly, comedians, anyone who would listen, with how she'd seen Ashley and Rex playing handsies, something rotten in the state of Denmark, and Perri pregnant with his child. Everyone laughed as though she were still telling jokes.

Conor taped her headshot over the cash register, in Magic Marker scrawling *Do not serve* across her grateful inscription to Rex.

"Biting the hand, Rosetta?" he said. "That's just *rude*."

She laughed uproariously.

19.

THE PROBLEM OF RACQUEL and her producer frustrated Joey as he labored at his corner of the IPO. Recording bogged down, and the latest tracks sounded full of unresolved tension.

Then he had a brainstorm. Racquel's boyfriend was an actor. Joey flew him to New York, had Byrne escort him to auditions, and himself found gigs to keep him busy and in town. Left on her own in Los Angeles, Racquel finally began an affair with Janos. Their collaboration turned smooth, if not noticeably faster, and sounded oh-so-sweet.

The capper occurred weeks later. The boyfriend, on the proceeds of doing an HBO promo that had him sitting awestruck in front of a TV screen that washed his face with transcendent light, returned without warning to L.A., surprised Racquel in bed with Janos and savagely beat her (Janos fled unscathed). While she was getting patched up at Cedars, inspiration struck and she quavered into her microcassette recorder a plangent new song, *What You Do To Me*.

Joey taped it over the phone and played it for Rex.

Rex listened tensely and barked, *"Perri!"*

Perri bustled in and Joey played it again.

"It's *gorgeous*," she declared.

"Sheer fucking *gravy*," said Rex, transported. "Girl's a *genius!*"

"Our first single," Joey said. "Number One, *guaranteed*."

He then turned his attention to his other act. The Come-Ons was a band made up of four teenage boys. Gaining in high school a following throughout Chicagoland, they deferred college to get serious about their music. Joey discovered them when, flying in for a week of showcases, he caught their performance at the Aragon Ballroom. He signed them on the spot.

He played Rex their new demo, *Curb It, Girl*. Rex crinkled his eyes as he listened.

"Who's singing?"

"Ramie? The sexy one?"

"Catchy."

"*Classic* hook. Rex, they're ready: Ready to go onstage in New York, ready to go into the studio. It's time to get product out. Do it *now*, we'll have it for the IPO."

"What's your plan?"

"Bring 'em in for a showcase at The Altar." The Altar was an old gothic church on Sixth Avenue below 23rd Street controversially turned into a disco. "Get the record companies in, they'll fall over each other—pay for a record *and* money upfront."

"Do it if it doesn't cost us anything."

Joey talked to their parents. It startled them that their sons' big-time New York managers wanted them to pay for the trip but, as loving fathers and mothers with no desire to kill a dream, they complied.

In the course of an antic night on the town with his old friend Klaus, The Altar's promoter, Joey struck a deal for a

Friday show: He could paper the house, while The Altar would pocket the liquor receipts. The band would get nothing except buzz beyond price.

"They go in and lay the crowd waste," Joey told Rex, "we've accomplished everything I wanted."

"I'm nervous, Joey. Prove me wrong."

Sneaking cash from the club (with Conor's and Frank's collusion), Joey commissioned a poster that showed the boys pouting like models who weren't getting along and hired a crew to plaster it to every wall in Manhattan. He sent Byrne out onto the streets to distribute free passes to hip-looking passers-by, and himself went to LaGuardia with the stretch and met the boys. Checking into the Omni Park Hotel (the cheap wing, unchanged since the Fifties), they evaded recognition by trotting across the sidewalk with heads lowered, then came by the office, gawky kids in torn jeans and shirts that gave artful hints of knee, thigh and nipple.

"Rex, we made it!" they boomed.

After *oohing* and *ahhing* at Tintinella's gold records and at the Thai food set out in the conference room, they listened earnestly as Rex spoke about ancillary rights, then went out to accomplish what they came to town determined to do.

This they did with help from a gentleman who, apparently reading their minds, approached them on Seventh Avenue. After they came to terms, the gentleman ducked around the corner into Original Ray's, where he patiently shook oregano into rolling paper and wrapped it tight. He sold the resulting mighty joint to them for $20. The boys returned to the Omni thrilled to have scored drugs in the Big Apple, though one or two later carped at the quality of New York weed.

But Charlie, the drummer, actually blamed its potency for what happened when they strolled through Times Square later. They came upon a man pushing playing cards around the top of a cardboard box. A small crowd was watching, one onlooker winning a fistful of cash by wagering which card, turned over, would prove to be the red one.

Charlie observed, grasped the principles, took out one of the five crisp $100 banknotes in his wallet and slapped it down.

Frowning, the man lifted the C-note to the sky.

"Man, this bill is *counterfeit!*" he said. "Show me something good!"

But the next bill also turned out to be fake.

"Man, where'd you *get* these?" the man asked.

"The bank," Charlie said in a strangled voice.

"Saw *you* coming!"

All five turned out to be counterfeit. Charlie was stunned.

"You done got taken," the man said kindly, tucking the evidence away. "Bad luck, bro."

The box collapsed and the man melted away.

"Oh, wow," said Charlie. He checked his wallet. Had he dreamed it? He checked his wallet again. "Oh, wow."

Joey persuaded Conor to build a simple set for the concert, as he had for many a cabaret act. Shopping on Canal Street yielded a quantity of twelve-foot plastic tubes. In the wide part of his building's entry hall he spray-painted them silver, liberally sprinkled glitter and rigged a base, ending up with what looked like disco prison bars.

The day of the concert Frank helped walk them over. On a side street down from The Altar, they passed an empty funeral parlor with a dusty *For Rent* sign in a window.

Conor couldn't resist, for all that he wasn't speaking to Frank.

"Perfect," he said. "We should turn it into a comedy club and call it The Last Laugh."

That night nerves had The Come-Ons throwing up before

their set. Rex arrived with Ashley on his arm (Perri pleaded her pregnancy), pushed through the crowd of people waving free passes and—being without one himself—was turned away at the door. He was livid until Joey ran out to vouch for him.

A DJ played dance music for hours, but at last The Come-Ons went on and *killed*. Prancing in their disco jail beneath the stone vaults, they led off with a tame version of *Curb It, Girl* and went through the rest of their energetic playlist before returning to a wild, no-holds-barred rendition, Ramie shimmying, wiggling and yelping. The crowd went crazy.

"Thought you were going to pull down your pants," Joey said later, still excited.

"Almost did," said Ramie, "but I thought that might be too much even for New York."

The crowd demanded several encores before accepting the DJ's beat again. A party raged in the VIP room up worn stone steps and through an arch. Rex failed to talk his way in—Joey had to rescue him—but once inside bubbled over.

"Great show, Joey. *Fantastic.*"

"All the record companies are here," Joey whispered. "Half the guys in here? A&R."

Next morning Joey showed up at work white with exhaustion, but serene even so. He moved uncharacteristically slowly, reserving his energy like a man who's been making love the whole night long. He read the trades while sipping coffee and crumbling a muffin and letting his telephone ring.

Finally he blotted his lips, wiped crumbs off his desk and picked up the phone.

"*Yo?*" he inquired.

It was Capitol Records offering $25,000 to release *Curb It, Girl* as a single.

"A *single?* Hector, that's *insulting*. A fucking *single* for a major act with an album's worth of original material? Were you *there* last night, Hector? They rocked the house! And you want to put out a single, see what happens, like they're one-hit wonders? This offer's so inadequate I can't even pass it on to the boys. When my phone's ringing off the hook? *Not* acceptable."

He slammed down the receiver.

"Best feeling I ever had," he reported. "Hanging up on fucking Capitol Records! A *single,* can you imagine? *Damn,* that felt good!"

But the next time his phone rang it was the nervous student promoter of a rock concert at Brooklyn College (he got short shrift). The call after that wanted an address for sending a demo tape. The call after that reminded him about his Macy's bill.

The Come-Ons' parents wired money to bring their boys home.

20.

CONOR'S SILENT TREATMENT of Frank stretched unto the day Rex got his first proofs of the Gag Reflex, Inc. prospectus. He had Byrne call Conor to the office. When he arrived, passing his partner without a word, Rex installed him in one Breuer chair and then, crooking a finger at the bullpen, put Frank in the other.

"Lucky people, look what papa's got for you," he said, turning from the open carton on his credenza. "Hot off the press, warm like bread from the oven: Form *S-fucking-1*." He handed them each an oversized book whose paper cover was densely printed in small type highlighted with cautions in red.

Conor said, "Shit, I'm afraid to look."

"Not ticking, anyway," said Frank.

This won a pro forma smile from Rex. "Page 37 should ease your fears," he told them.

They duly turned there, and their eyes widened.

"Executive Stock Options," Rex murmured benignly. "What's it say, Conor, 20,000 shares, four bucks a share? Frank, for you, I think 10,000?"

"Thank you," said Frank.

"Told you I'd make you rich!"

"We getting close?" Conor asked.

"Could hear any moment that I've satisfied the regulators," Rex told him. "Am I *pooped!* Perri can tell you, I've been servicing the SE-fucking-C day and *night*. They're smoking a cigarette right now.

"But there's one thing bothers me. My manager not talking to my assistant? Can you imagine how that makes me feel?"

"Yes, as a matter of fact," Frank said.

"Rex, got a little problem myself," said Conor.

"Tell me."

"This phone forwarding *sucks*. It eats away at me. You hired *me* to run that store, and I'm breaking my ass trying to do it smooth as shit, no coke in the bathrooms, crowds of happy laughing customers—but *I* have to transfer *my* telephone *here*, let *my* customers talk to *you?*"

"Conor," said Frank.

"Not talking to you," Conor said, facing Rex. "But notice I'm not going behind *your* back."

"You're serious," Rex said.

"Yessir."

Taking a prospectus, Rex balanced it on the tips of ten fingers. The way he held it made it look weighty.

"See this?"

"Yeah . . ."

"What would you say this is?"

"Um, that's your prospectus, Rex."

"*This* is the weigh-in before the fight. We're naked in here, Conor, stripped and on the scales, every fucking piece of equipment we got on display. 'Here we are,' we're saying, 'come and get us.'

"Now, facts are lovely things. Sure they are. *Love* 'em. But the *fact* is, I own a sewer on First Avenue—and I want to sell *stock* in it?" A lopsided grin appeared. "Should get my head examined, right? Where do I get the *balls?*

"So *my* job is to conjure up a vision out of the pathetic *facts* you guys wallow in all day long, make 'em see—not my 97-pound shithole bar—but the huge fucking man-mountain entertainment *empire* we'll be five years from now."

It was the dog-and-pony show Siggy was taking him around town to perform, flatteringly put on for the benefit of two.

"This book gives anyone who wants it the chance to poke at us, look at our teeth, feel our muscles, bend us over and look up our ass. They go over the projections, see the pictures of Freddie Prinze, Andy Kaufman— *Damn* if they don't start seeing what I *want* 'em to see. Lo and behold, they look at Racquel and see *Madonna*, look at *Hank*, see the young Johnny Carson.

"OK, so they put in their money, what do they get?"

"Wallpaper?" Frank suggested.

Rex ignored him.

"They get a piece of our *magic*. Because what business are we in? When you come down to it, wouldn't you say we're in the business of *magic?*

"Life takes a dump on you, come to the Gag Reflex, roar with fucking laughter, you're purified and *free*. We sell being free—being alive—*magic*. Can't keep this to ourselves! People need it! Time to sell stock to raise the money to build the new clubs, fish those new clubs for the new stars to make the new records, new TV shows, new movies. It's shooting monkeys in a barrel when *we own the barrel.*

"Because if there's global consensus on any one thing, one demand common to every man, woman and child alive on Earth today, it's this: I *must* be entertained. I *must* be fucking well *entertained!* Give me laughs, noise, lights, something—

anything—to lift the burden of my sorry little self and fill this scary blank called *life* I don't know what to do with. *Fill* it for me! *Kill* it for me!"

His face shining, Rex softened his voice.

"That is the cry of mankind. And the cry of mankind will never be denied.

"Wallpaper? Anyone not *100%* with me, my advice, get out now, 'cause so long as you're on board, when I say fucking *pull,* you fucking *pull* your fucking *oar.*

"Conor: After the IPO, there'll be too much going on in here to bother about reservations, we'll turn 'em back to the club, figure something out. But till then, every cover charge counts, OK? Meanwhile I don't want my assistant and my manager not getting along because of some stupid turf thing. Trust me?"

"OK, Rex," Conor said.

"Frank, you'll go back to Conor's?"

Frank nodded dumbly.

"Kiss and make up?"

Conor darted across the gap between their chairs, planted one on Frank's cheek.

"You can do better," said Rex.

They embraced, their lips met, tongues touched.

"People, if we're family, if we stick together even when the vultures are picking at our *guts,* no fucking *way* can we fail!" Wiping his face, Rex stood up and slid open his door. "Shit, I'm wiped out. Next I'll be getting larger than life."

"A legend in your own mind," Conor said, getting to his feet.

"That's funny," said Rex, calling, "Ashley, am I right, that's funny?"

"Sure it is," she told him.

"I started out in novelties," Rex went on, "and if coffee

mugs could be my life, I'd be comfortable today. But I had a vision. That's why I'm putting us through hell."

Having thus shared more than ever before, he closed his door and got on the phone.

"Lordy," said Conor. *"Wow!"*

"He's my man," said Joey.

"I saw him first," said Perri.

Ashley said, "He'll pull it off."

After Conor left, Rex hung up and gestured Frank back into his office.

"Frank, I know your intentions about helping Conor are good, but think how it looks to *him*: We're the big bad office telling him what to do and how to do it, and though you and I and even *he* knows you're here to make things better for him, to him it looks like you're with *us*. And—*c'mon*—you don't want to *compete*, you two."

Frank could of course dismiss any possibility that *Rex* could offer insight concerning his relationship with Conor.

"You and Perri—" he started.

"C'mon, that's *different*," Rex declared without explanation. "Don't think I didn't hear your *wallpaper* crack. Need to know, Frank, are you with me?

"Wait, I heard you chime in, but words are cheap, I should know. Be honest, do you *mean* it? I know I ask a lot. It's OK if that *yes* is sincere, but I'm telling you, if you're with me only 'cause you want to be with *Conor*—put aside what that means in terms of business, I'm telling you, it'll rot your soul."

He watched Frank for a long moment, and rose to his feet.

"OK, can't say I didn't try."

"How can I help loving the guy?" thought Frank as he said, "I'm with you, Rex. With you all the way."

Smiling broadly, Rex pumped his hand.

Frank moved back to Conor's. He proposed sealing their

reunion with sex. That didn't happen, but things were sweet and without conflict between them. They slept in each other's arms, were especially considerate of each other.

It was nice, though it felt less like being the life of their relationship than its afterlife.

21.

ACCEPTING ASHLEY'S INVITATION to spend an April weekend at her father's, Rex and Perri sped out of town in a rented Jaguar XJ-S with the top down. Passing between the towers of the George Washington Bridge, they found a fast road north. Rex worked out his anger at The Come-Ons fiasco and his other troubles in the way he shifted gears and took the curves, while Perri sat beside him scarfed and trying to duck the wind.

High on Rex's weekend agenda was yanking an investment out of Mr. Parrish.

"That doesn't work," he shouted, "I'll have to bite the bullet."

"Call Tintinella?"

"Beg her on my *knees* to buy a private placement."

"But Black, why *not?* You made millions for her. Best investment she could make," Perri said staunchly.

"Lets Germano know I'm up shit creek."

"Oh, *pride.*"

"Plus she'll probably want what I owe her first. She's that way."

"You owe *her?*"

"Germano's fault, greedy son of a bitch, don't get me started. She's in town Monday. Comes to it, what I'll do is pay her her money, then *boom!* pitch her hard. She take ten units, we're home free."

And flipping the driver the bird, he gunned past a truck.

The dissolution of his partnership with Germano was finalized at a day-long closing with their respective legal teams. The lawyers argued, initialed reams of documents, signed multitudinous side-letters (after negotiating endless changes), ritually wrote each other numerous small checks, sent out for lunch, bickered, broke for dinner and signed some more, all while Rex and Germano needled each other about their respective prospects.

Finally it was done, except that Rex (or, as he claimed, his attorneys) had forgotten about a piddling $6,000 due Tintinella as a refund on revenues he realized on one of her records after he and Germano with a handshake had broken up. Everybody agreed he could pay her later.

It slipped his mind until a stiffish letter from her attorney arrived, which Rex finessed by calling her and pleading hurt feelings that an honest oversight (and one so tiny!) should be referred to lawyers, and she had disclaimed any knowledge, and there Rex gingerly left it, intending to pay up just as soon as a spare $6,000 came his way.

Spring was late, but an uncanny tender green was beginning to creep over the hills.

"How much do you owe her, Black?"

"What is it, $6,000?"

"Do we even *have* $6,000?"

"Sure, the weekend."

"That'll bounce the paychecks!"

"So it will, Perri, so it will. Got a better idea? Maybe sell the baby or something?"

"*Black!*"

"Perri, my *dream* depends on this. But unless Ashley's dad's an *idiot*, it won't come to that."

Soon they were navigating winding roads that made Perri fear they were lost.

"Black, pull into that station and ask."

"Know why women like to ask directions?" Rex remarked, speeding onwards. "'Cause that way you're always doing what someone tells you to. So fucking *dependent*."

A few minutes later by way of apology he said, "Listen, everyone can cash their checks at the club."

"OK, Black, I didn't say a thing."

"Goddam *fuck!*"

Downshifting, he shot past a Caddy whose ancient driver was rocking the wheel like a cradle.

Ashley's father lived in — apparently never stirred from — the old family place in Tuxedo Park. That her great-grandfather had been a Morgan partner Rex knew, but what the present-day financial facts of life for them were he wasn't sure. But he had his suspicions.

They were admitted through the town gates. Their eyes widened as they drove roads from which enormous old houses receded into the peace of high-priced greenery.

"My God, Black, it's like a reservation for mansions."

"Old money," he bit off. "Nothing like it."

They found the Parrish drive and climbed half a mile alongside stone walls before achieving a hilltop where stood a monstrously big house in Richardsonian Romanesque, three and four stone stories artfully massed beneath towering chimneys and a block-long roofline of slate.

"This I don't fucking *believe!*" Rex gasped. "Megahouse!"

"I'm nervous," Perri said.

"Lady, we have *arrived!*"

Rex parked in front, then, suddenly uncertain, backed over the gravel to a different spot. Getting out, he looked up at the façade. It loomed in blank disregard. Perri labored to her feet.

"I don't know," he said. "Ring the bell?"

He mounted to the flagstone terrace and pulled a chain that set an interior bell to ringing merrily, before retreating a few steps. Nothing happened. He knocked. Nothing. Perri sat down heavily on a marble bench. Two men were raking a distant lawn, and Rex could sense Perri about to suggest asking *them.*

"Hey, guys, over here," came a familiar raspy yell. Rex turned and saw a cottage, the house in miniature, and Ashley striding across the intervening lawn. "Perri, glad you could make it!"

Perri thought it the *oddest* weekend. Great-Granddad's mansion was shut up and Ashley's father lived in the old chauffeur's cottage. It was a solid and roomy stone bungalow, entirely charming, but made for a picture hard to decipher.

That evening Ashley gave them a tour of "the big house" (put that way, it sounded like Sing-Sing). It was amazing: The rooms were built to a scale that appeared to require inhabitants ten feet tall. "Makes me feel *tiny,*" Perri said happily, "and it's been awhile." There was a great hall, a series of reception rooms surrounding a glass-roofed palm court, a monumental staircase, two bedroom wings (with another for servants) and, grandest of all, a music room. Ashley pointed out the gallery where a Victrola used to be set up after dinner with a footman stationed beside it to turn over the 78s. The rooms were superbly furnished with European antiques, and beautifully maintained.

Rex started the tour in confusion, feeling as small and bewildered as a child. But in the lofty library — where tiers of bronze-railed balconies ascended to Tiffany skylights—he said, "I get it, *we're* the giants! *Have* to be, to occupy the giant's castle. Ash, I had no idea. Why don't you live here?"

"Who wants to live in a museum?" she said. "Daddy hated it growing up, and I don't see the use myself. Should have torn it down when we had the chance. Now we're going to have to give it away or something."

Ashley's mother was long out of the picture. Mr. Parrish was a pleasant but aloof person, solicitous of his daughter's guests' comfort and tastes—he cooked the meals—but himself somehow veiled. His eyes never quite met theirs, and though he spilled over with small talk, it was never so personal as to include them or his daughter or himself, much less Ashley's career or Rex's business. Rex was flummoxed.

After Saturday's dinner of shad roe, Perri whispered, "Black, do they even *have* money? Or did they *lose* it?"

"Oh, they have it. *This* charm? *This* vagueness? Fifty million, *minimum*."

"Hope you're right."

On Sunday afternoon Rex took advantage of Ashley's showing Perri the local antique stores (driving a battered old station wagon that scandalized him) to sit down with Mr. Parrish and the *Times* on his little back porch. The view from the big house took in the Hudson Valley. Mr. Parrish's cottage overlooked a walled yard of clotheslines.

"Quite a daughter you have there, Mr. Parrish," Rex began.

"Piece of work," her father agreed, folding the *Business and Finance* section.

"Big help to me. She's told you about our company, of course? And the IPO?"

"Mentioned it." Mr. Parrish smiled. "You're a brave man, Mr. Black."

Rex put off considering what he might mean.

"We're coming on the market soon, but there's time for one last round of private placements. Units of 3,000 shares, priced at $10,000. That's 3.33 bucks a share, as opposed to the $5-*plus* we'll come to market at. Don't know if you've followed how popular comedy clubs have become?"

Mr. Parrish was exquisitely patient. Heard Rex out to the bitter end, then said, "Wish you luck. Lots of it."

"*Nothing,*" Rex complained to Perri. "Gave me back *nothing*. Wishes me luck, peers through dime-store reading glasses at stock tables for half an hour, asks do I want to see his fucking *dovecote*. Perri, tell me frankly: Have I lost it?"

She reassured him.

That evening, Rex bit the bullet. Borrowing Mr. Parrish's study, he phoned Tintinella at home in Ojai. While he waited for them to find her he idly tried the desk drawers. Every one of them was locked. She came on the line, heard him out, said she looked forward to talking about it over dinner the next day and, oh, by the way, didn't he owe her $6,000?

"Have it for you at dinner, Tinny."

"Love you, Rex. Cashier's check, OK?"

"Only the best for you."

He was limp, drained. No reason. Couldn't have been nicer, whole thing took five minutes.

Then he called the club and listened to New York's nervous layered buzz and the chink of glasses for a long minute before Conor came on.

"*Hey*-ya, Rex."

"Took your time."

"Busy night."

"Sell out?"

"Oh yeah."

"One thing: I know the deposit goes into *operating* now, but this one time I need it in the *corporate* account. Got that?"

"Got it: Corporate account."

"Have a deposit slip?"

"Some right here."

"So how much we talking, roughly?"

"Should be $12,000 and change."

"Thataboy!"

In bed Rex had a final complaint, for Perri's ears alone.

"*Great-Granddad* would have whipped out his checkbook. Those Morgan guys? Could *smell* the ground floor. *Great-Granddad* would have taken one look at the Gag Reflex and stolen it out from under me!

"Didn't call 'em robber barons for nothing! Skipped a generation with Junior. He's *pathetic.*"

22.

WHILE REX AND PERRI were fighting city-bound traffic Monday morning, with Ashley hunched in the Jag's putative backseat next to Perri's new antique milk can, the ADP messenger dropped off the weekly satchel of paychecks. Joey foraged for his and ran to the bank. Perri came in exclaiming at the peace of the countryside, while Rex went on to drop off Ashley.

Joey rushed back in with a worried face.

"Frank, the bank wouldn't cash my check!" he said, flipping Exhibit A onto his desk.

"*What?*"

"Said the payroll account's empty!"

"That's absurd," Frank said. "The wire must have hit by now."

"I owe rent."

"Hold on, Joey, I'll fix it." Frank punched the telephone keypad.

Byrne asked, "How do you keep them from bouncing, anyway?"

"Wire funds from the operating account to payroll every Monday morning," Frank answered. "Elementary."

"Revolutionary," sniffed Byrne.

Perri looked over. "Frank's very efficient," she said.

"That's what I mean," Byrne said.

"Payroll is sacred," Frank declared, then, into the phone, "Hi, Rita, it's Frank at the Gag Reflex. Rita, I brought over a wire transfer earlier, but ... *Empty* ...? Deposit went to *corporate?* Oh, no, someone goofed up this end. I'll run a check over right away, we need it in payroll. Thanks, Rita."

Rex strode in, the relaxed country squire in soft-collared suede. Joey waved that morning's Liz Smith at him.

"See Tintinella's in town?"

"We dine this very evening."

"Hitting her up for a private placement?"

"Soon's I pay off that stupid 6K I owe her," said Rex, picking up the corporate checkbook and making out a check to Cash. "Frank, do me a favor, run this to the bank and buy a cashier's check, $6,000, order of Tintinella Limited."

"We don't have that much in corporate," Frank told him. "Not after —"

"Don't tell me," said Rex. "Oh, *please* don't tell me. Called Conor last night myself, told him very clear: 'This week put it in *corporate.' Shit*, if he didn't do a simple thing like that!"

"He did it," Frank said, "or someone did."

"So what's the problem?"

"He didn't tell me."

"Gee, maybe because that's *my money* we're talking about?"

"I mean we need it in payroll. You've got an $8,000 payroll to cover, Rex, what with the tax payment, plus we owe a good $3,000 for liquor. We had a great weekend, but that leaves just over —"

"*Payroll?*"

"Rex, that's not your money, it's *wages*: My money, Joey's money —"

"Holy shit," Rex said flatly. His face was granite, the triangles under his eyes dead white. He waited.

"You want me to bounce the paychecks?" Frank asked. "I don't think I can do that."

Rex turned his palms upward.

"Heaven *forfend!* No problem, sorry I *asked.* Too much to expect anyone works for me to wait a few days."

"*I'll* get the cashier's check," said Perri.

"Oh, but would it be *right?* Mr. Fiscal Integrity has *doubts.*"

"Really, Black, *I'll* go."

"Golly, but if Mr. Honesty Incarnate thinks it's *wrong?*" Rex stood over him. "Frank, what you're doing is a huge fucking mistake. Tintinella's a lock for a hundred K — *if* I pay her what I owe her. Pay six, get a *hundred,* don't you *get* it?"

"There has to be some other way — "

"Oh, the word's come down!" said Rex. "From on high!"

"Could you give her a post-dated check? Or wait, if *her* check clears overnight — "

Rex scoured his ear with a pinky.

"Am I hearing things? *Tintinella* we're talking about. She could buy you and sell you a million times over, my friend."

"OK, *my* check you can hold, let's see who else's, maybe it adds up — "

"Holy *shit,*" said Rex. "Simple trip to the bank!"

He stormed into his office and slammed the door shut. Golgotha. The door came off the track. Furiously he wrestled it back on, slipped it open an inch and said in a small, pained voice, "Perri."

Perri went in and closed the door.

Joey eased towards his cubbyhole. Everybody got busy.

Rex yanked open his door and stormed out.

"Need to concentrate on my *pitch,* and you give me *this?*" he said. "Frank, we all make mistakes, but the way to get over them is to take some goddam *responsibility*. I need people who take the blame when they fuck up—take the blame, feel like shit, pick up and go on. 'Cause if *they* don't feel like shit, *I* feel like shit, and *that's* bad for business."

"I take responsibility when I'm at fault," Frank said.

"Better you take it when *I* am," said Rex. "Just kidding. Now go. *Chop chop.* Cashier's check, six K."

Frank didn't move. Perri hovering like a bodyguard, Rex sank onto the corner of his desk and spoke softly.

"Frank, do you like your job?"

"That's just it, Rex, I *love* my job, and I'm trying to do it, but it carries certain responsibilities, like seeing to it that your employees and the IRS get paid—"

"Thing about jobs is, you have a *boss*. And when the bossman says—"

"Perri, could we possibly stretch out the liquor bills?"

"Frank, are you seriously suggesting I let Tintinella know that six fucking grand *breaks* me? Same as kissing the IPO goodbye!

"Meant to talk to you about this, anyway. Cashing paychecks at the club gave us a nice *float*: Gave 'em their checks Monday, they held on to 'em till the weekend. *Your* way loses us what we need *most* right now, which is flexibility, plus now they *expect* their checks to be good."

"Could you go to Joe D.? *Any* interest rate might be worth it."

Rex went bug-eyed.

"Frank!" Perri said. "How dare you!"

"Guy would kill me soon as look at me," said Rex. "What's *he* care? Anything happen to me, he's got my *club*. Frank, I literally don't get it. Perri, do you get it?"

"No, Black," she said sadly, "I don't get it."

Rex strode towards his office, Perri following. From the

cross, he wailed, "Do I have to be Charles Atlas, hold up the whole fucking *world?*" before slamming the door home.

Frank woke up Conor and learned that indeed he'd put the weekend receipts into the corporate account.

"And you didn't tell me? Conor, we're a team."

"Yeah, Dolls, but the same one? So some checks bounce? I don't get the hoopla."

"After a certain point we share responsibility," Frank said.

"You are so naïve," Conor informed him.

"I admit, it's built-in. Dammit, what should I *do?* I love this job."

"Do what you want. You will anyway."

"What's best for you?"

"Leave *me* out of it, I can deal. Shit, like *your* job? This is my *career.*"

"I can swallow a lot, but—"

"The way Rex is doing it? Way it's done, Dolls."

"Rex is a shark: Has to devour celebs or die," Frank said. "Doesn't *celeb* even sound like a soluble fat?"

"Sharks do what they got to do. I'm something of one myself."

"Don't be such a tough guy, Conor."

"I keep it simple, Dolls: I do what Rex tells me. By yourself on this one. I'd just go get him his check."

Conor hung up.

Frank stood up and looked around. *"Who are these people?"* he wondered. *"How did I get here?"* At Rex's threshold he announced, "OK, Rex, I'm going to the bank."

"Doing the right thing," Rex called, his teeth sparkling. "It's for the greater good."

Frank went down the street and bought the cashier's check, answering the teller's eager questions about the IPO while alarm bells rang inside him.

Rex carefully folded the check into his wallet.

"Thanks, boyfriend, knew you'd come through," he said. "Sit down a minute."

Frank sat down. Perri took the other chair.

"Been thinking 'bout what you said. Put aside how I feel about anyone saying, 'This *one* thing that's crucial? That's the *one* thing I won't do!' Let me explain what's going on. You're right I have to pay people their salaries."

"Yes?"

"*Absolutely*," said Rex. "But I can't help thinking you don't grasp what I'm trying to do here. I mean the big picture."

"I think I do."

"But have you thought that if things go as I hope and trust they will, and as my fucking investment bankers— Oh, excuse my language, won't you, please? I know it's rough on you."

"Sure, Rex."

"So kind," said Rex. "—as they assure me things *will* go, year from now it won't be 20, 25 people I'll be struggling to pay, it'll be ten *times* that—"

"I know."

"—on its way to a *hundred* times that. People making good money, paying taxes on jobs that don't even exist yet."

"I hope so."

"But to get there from where we are today, we have to be careful, precise, coordinated. Remember that nursery rhyme, *The House That Jack Built*? How's it go?"

Frank looked blank.

"I know, Black," said Perri. "*This is the cat/That killed the rat/That ate the malt/That lay in the house that Jack built.*"

"Exactly," said Rex. "'*For want of a fucking nail, the kingdom was lost.*' See what I'm driving at? Big fish eating the little fish? Everything connects!

"Paying Tintinella's just pounding in a threepenny nail:

Nothing! But without it, the Gag Reflex folds like a−like a−"

"House of cards?" Frank thought. Out loud he said, "I understand, Rex: It's actually a lesson in thrift."

"Know what scares me? The day Wall Street hands me my money: 'OK, here's your bread, now *deliver.*' That's the *real* fucking nightmare.

"Frank, I'm curious: Don't you *want* to succeed?" Rex's eyes narrowed while Frank considered. "Fuck, have to *think* about it?"

"There's a price too high−"

"Black, I don't feel well," Perri said.

"Oh, the fucking catfights we're in for! (Hang on, Perri.) New people staking out turf, ratting each other out." He pointed across the bullpen. "Punching through soon as it happens, take over next door. Double our space, but even so." His voice softened. "Frank, I give an order, to have it questioned, that introduces an element of confusion, follow? You made a mistake."

"Yes, I did," Frank said. "Of course, in similar circumstances I'd do the same, but that, too, would be a mistake."

Rex's mouth worked. "You and I, we can't communicate, can we?"

"My first mistake was to go to work for you."

"That so?"

"But it's not personal, or if it is, it's not you."

"Then all I can say is, poor Conor−poor, *poor* Conor. You make a lot of mistakes."

"I hope two weeks' notice will undo this one."

"Should," said Rex. "Unless it's *another?* I'm sorry, I really am. And the timing doesn't help. Sends a signal."

"Sorry."

"So be it."

Frank was dismissed. Perri closed the door behind him, but not before he heard, "Stabbed in the fucking *back!*"

The bullpen had an atmosphere as Frank sat down at his desk and, by reflex, not consciously looking for anything, opened and closed its drawers.

Byrne said, "Your problem is, Rex is succeeding."

"Rex is something of a con man," Frank informed him.

"Like, *duh*. But what's he conned *you* out of?"

"My lover, maybe?" Frank thought.

"Least he's *our* con man," Joey declared. "Taken everything he's done to get us this far, but once it happens we're *set*."

"Can't cheat an honest man," Byrne put in.

Frank meanwhile pulled out the manila envelope Rex gave him to hide from the auditors.

Rex saw it and marched out.

"*Terrific!* Forgot about those fuckers! We'll shred 'em for my tickertape parade! Those and a few other pieces of paper. Think I'm *stupid?* Go ask Wall Street how *stupid* I am! Not going to the SEC, are you?"

"No," said Frank.

"Go with my blessing, they won't fucking *care*. Badmouth me all over town, I'm immune to anything *you* can do. Know why? Because *I* make people feel *alive!* And *you* make 'em feel *dead!* You smell of duty, the fine print, standing back with a hanky to your nose watching the rest of us take a shit every day of our lives, and if – God forbid! – you ever find out it's every man for himself, anybody gets between you and what you want, got to let them have it right between the legs, fuck *them* before they fuck *you* – "

Frank slammed the office door behind him.

Wrenching it open, Rex followed.

" – it's so long, you're *outa* here! *Later!* It's every man for himself that keeps you *honest*, asswipe!"

Rex threw the envelope at the elevator as Frank boarded it. Its doors closed in a blizzard of guest checks.

Back in the office, Rex said, "*Fuck!* Known he was in it for the paycheck, would have fired him long ago. All I ask is a little belief. Aren't I entitled to a little *belief*? A little fucking *loyalty*?"

Over dinner Tintinella agreed to kick in $100,000 for the ten units Rex suggested.

"Why not?" she said, stuffing his check in her cleavage. "I've got a little mad money."

"Bread cast upon the waters," Rex assured her. "Get it back a hundredfold."

She gave him a peculiar look, but said nothing.

Meanwhile Perri called Frank at Conor's. He answered with a leaden, "Hello?"

What he'd done was sinking in. That office so exotic, so fun? Two more weeks, then gone to him forever. And why, over *money*? If Rex mishandled *his* puny salary, he didn't care, so why should he care about anyone else's? But he sensed the issues were larger, that pride was in play—his, in such mundane accomplishments as making sure paychecks were good, versus Rex's, in having a crew that at his command would willingly—in his parlance—*bend over.*

All Frank could do was watch TV, though nothing registered except (surreally) an A&E stand-up segment taped at the Gag Reflex, comedians braying and strutting in front of the *tchotchkes* that once made Conor's place so homey.

And if working with Conor hadn't brought them closer, Frank sensed his quitting would cleave them apart.

What Perri had to say was, "Black says you don't need to come in again. I'll mail your last check."

"OK, Perri," he said. "Nice working with you. Good luck."

"Same here," she said. "Please don't cash it for a week."

23.

REX COUNTED on the windfall from Tintinella to carry him through to the IPO, but $100,000 is peanuts for a company in the throes of going public, particularly when the target date for hitting the market is shadowy, even receding.

"My finger's in the wind," Siggy assured him. "Got a sixth sense about these things, you'll see. Market's a tad weaker than I like right now. Just hold on."

The windfall soon eroded to $60,000, to $40,000, to $20,000. The club, though doing better than ever, couldn't make up for the outflow. Rex hit up everybody he had or hadn't tried before, including his mother's bridge partners at the Boreal Shores Country Club, where his appeal failed signally.

"You don't get old if you fall for every sucker pitch you hear," his mother pointed out with amusement.

"*Ma!*"

His existing investors were antsy — impatient for the IPO to place a valuation on their investment, even eager to pull out some cash. Half Rex's time went to pleading with them to be patient. He assured them Racquel's upcoming CD was *hot*, that Hank was on the verge of national breakout — hang in there, he'd make them *rich*.

One frazzled Tuesday in May—another day of no apparent forward progress—Rex went home steaming with frustration. He helped Perri settle in front of the TV where she could spoon pudding while watching old movies, and as the light weakened pulled on his Adidas and dashed across town on 90th Street, at Fifth Avenue heading north on the Park Drive. Rex was a fine runner, doing his comfortable six-mile circuit of Central Park in 41, 42 minutes. The inviting curves and hills were emptying out, and the roadway was free of cars, except for a few illicitly racing. He began to breathe hard and free.

He was coming down the West Drive pounding out his tension, thinking of nothing, when three runners hogging the wrong lane—*his* lane—came at him. The one in the middle, a tiny woman in a baseball cap, was making for him head-on.

Let her follow the rules, dammit! Fuck if he'd *move!*

Rex went straight ahead.

Then he recognized one of the men, then the other, and when, at the last second, the woman looked up and stepped aside, Rex recognized *her*.

"Gather round, everybody," he said next morning, clapping his hands as he entered the office. His face was radiant. "The gods gave us a sign last night!"

Perri that morning had the secret smile of the Mona Lisa. Rex evinced no impatience while Byrne and Joey and his new assistant, Trish, disengaged from the phones. A certain self-importance informed his pose.

"OK," said Rex. "Last night, I go for a run in Central Park?" He looked around. Everybody was politely expectant. "I'm going along and three assholes—two guys and a woman—come at me in *my* lane. 'Better fucking *move*,' I think. Put my head down and bull ahead.

"Then I recognize the bodyguard from the *Post*, then the

boyfriend, and when the woman gets out of my way, I realize it's fucking *Madonna! Herself!*

"People, I played chicken with Madonna—and I *won!*"

Laughing, he slammed his fist into his hand.

"*I* beat *her!* Madonna fucking *lost!* The gods are on *my* side! This deal is going through! Tell everyone," he said, going into his office. "I want *everybody* to know."

A little while later his private line rang.

"Rex? Si—" <static>

"Siggy! How *are* you?"

High on the list of Rex's recent frustrations was that he wasn't hearing from Siggy.

"—ne. Look—" <static> <static> "—delay. Not too long, I hope."

"Siggy, we've got the worst fucking connection. You in the Daimler? You're breaking up."

"—not a—" <static> <static> "—market, but—" <static>

"Siggy, I'm losing you!"

"—look different. In this business, you can't predict tomorrow."

"Siggy, could you repeat what you just said?"

"About postponing your IPO?"

The call dropped.

Rex hit the speed dials. No answer at Siggy's car phone. No answer at Siggy's private line. Maple Tree's main number bounced him among disembodied voices. He could raise no living soul.

Muttering that he'd be back, he muscled into his jacket and was out the door. Heedless of whether he might be seen, he jumped underground, riding the No. 3 to Wall Street, loping down Broad, darting into the lamplighted lane and dashing indoors to where Maple Tree's elevator stood open and dark. Using another, he rocketed upwards and stepped into Maple

Tree's lobby, forgetting to put on his company face. He looked worried.

There was no Persian rug and no Barbie. Instead, a man was pushing a wheeled bin filled with shredded paper over scuffed terrazzo.

"Where *is* everybody?" Rex asked, his voice echoing.

"*No habla ingles*," the man answered.

"Am I fucking *dreaming?*"

Siggy's office doors stood open. Rex went in. The vast room was empty but for a blue-smocked woman working a vacuum cleaner. Nail holes showed in the paneling.

Stunned, Rex looked out at Siggy's panorama. Office towers still accurately divided themselves into cells, boats still creased the harbor, planes and helicopters still strung the sky. Lady Liberty, the encouraging color of a dollar bill, sneered at him.

A man carrying a briefcase came in and peremptorily demanded, "Where's Brewster? What's happening?"

"You poor *schmuck*," said Rex with lifted lip. "You *sucker!* You *loser!*"

Blanching, the man whispered, "Is this a *nightmare?*"

Rex peered into the shark tank on his way out. It was empty, the carpeting shadowed with traffic patterns.

Downstairs he strode over to Broad Street to flag a cab. Empty ones went flying past him. A man downstream raising a finger, a taxi squealed to a halt and bore him away. Rex tried again. A cab swerved towards him, and two men stepped awkwardly around him and got in it.

"That's *my* fucking taxi!" he informed them, pummeling their shoulders. They appeared not to notice.

Rex gestured, he leapt, he whistled – to no avail. A rat shot out of the sewer onto the sidewalk and raced up his pants. He danced on one foot, the rat fell out and bounced back into the sewer, the whole thing happening within two seconds.

Finally he shouted *"Stop!"* at an empty passing Checker, its startled driver braked and Rex got in.

"What am I, chopped liver?"

"Didn't see you," the driver said.

They were heading up the West Side Highway when Madonna's newest hit *Who's That Girl* came on the radio. The driver turned up the volume. Rex put his face to the partition.

"Turn that shit *off*," he commanded. *"Hate* that slimy cunt. Whoever told her she could *sing?"*

The driver made it louder.

"Turn it *off*," Rex yelled.

The cab lurched to a halt and the driver turned around. There were scary squealings behind, and a crescendo of horns.

"I own this cab, mister. Get out."

"Can't get *out*, we're on the fucking *highway."*

"Out!"

The driver wrapped his arms around the wheel. Rex protested for a while, but the moment came when he did get out, cross the shoulder, step over the concrete barrier separating the highway from West Street and dart across four lanes of traffic with his arms raised, mocked by Madonna every step of the way.

He found an uptown bus and called Harshaw as soon as he reached the office.

"Who knows?" Harshaw reassured him languidly, his clock ticking at $350 an hour. "Maybe one of his young sharks did something not quite kosher, so Siggy —"

"Such as?"

"How would *I* know? Unless it's like last time —"

"Last time?"

"Feds claimed a dry-cleaning chain he underwrote was a money-laundering scheme," said Harshaw. "Like Siggy should know from *dry cleaning?* Took his suspension like a man, came out of that mess with Maple Tree."

"I thought Maple Tree was around for *years.* Those offices—"

"He'll figure things out, Rex, surface sooner than you think: Guy's a survivor."

These comments, Rex knew, would show up on Harshaw's monthly pro forma (he was withholding his actual bill until the IPO filled the coffers) as a $70 item annotated ".2 hours, telephone conference with Mr. Black re: securities issues."

24.

FRANK WAS DEPRESSED and at loose ends for weeks – in mourning as though a friend had died. He adopted Conor's hours. When Conor got home he'd find him watching a movie on HBO; they dined on something from the deli across Bleecker – roast-beef sandwiches, macaroni salad, Entenmann's coffeecake – and woke up next day to the same movie being repeated. They began to get on each other's nerves in a new way.

One day Conor said, "Dolls, you better get a job."

By all means. Frank had rent to pay, too. But couldn't he salvage something from his Gag Reflex experience? Parlay it into something more vital, more rewarding than a return to proofreading? Something that would keep him in Conor's professional orbit, even give him another chance to fit him with a yoke of intimacy?

"Conor, remember your crack about turning that funeral home into a comedy club? 'The Last Laugh'?"

"Oh shit."

"Been thinking about it: It's actually a *great* idea – so *nutty* people would go for it. All anyone's thinking about these days is death. And that space is still for rent. Location's terrific, could get liquor-licensed easily. Help me write a business plan, and I'll look for the money and maybe we can run our own club together."

"I work for Rex."

"We'll invite him to fund it. Sell him half. Czar of two franchises? He'd love it."

"Business plan? Go ahead. But keep my name out of it."

Frank had marveled over Rex's business plan, especially the inexorable quarter-by-quarter march towards riches it laid out in black and white. After putting in some time at the New York Public Library's Business Division, he started putting the outlines of his own on paper.

One day the phone rang.

"Frank? Rosetta Stone. 'The Last Laugh'? What a *pisser!*"

"Who told you?"

"But get the entertainment angle right or people will be offended. And nail down that space, *fast*. Dance floor in the embalming room, did you think of *that?*"

Later Frank complained to Conor, "It was supposed to be confidential."

"Hey, I forgot, OK? Saw her around, she asked what you were up to. *Loves* the idea. She's smart, you should bring her on board."

So Frank had a partner, which, it turned out, was what he craved. If Conor was indifferent, Rosetta was fascinated. They got together for giddy brainstorming sessions where they decided on using toe-tag coat checks, memorial cards for menus, and on and on.

"Frank, we've *got* to get that space," she repeated one evening.

"Let's go knock on the door."

So under the most serene skies New York sees all year—

May's lofty maritime envelopments of blue—they ventured into that fragment of Dickens' London that Sixth Avenue south of 23rd Street represented in those days. Vast 19th-century department stores stood vacant or were used for warehouses or printing plants. Save for the line already forming outside The Altar, the neighborhood was deserted.

Their object was a gloomy stone building that looked like a Victorian gothic chapel. Its dusty *For Rent* sign seemed of Dickens' time, too.

Frank lifted the bronze head of a veiled woman and hit the striker. It resounded.

"So cool," said Rosetta.

"But no one home."

But someone was. The door was pulled open by a man in a loud shirt with gold medallions strung around his neck, the rest of the sandwich he was chewing in his hand. He looked at them expressionlessly.

"Hello," Frank said, "we saw the *For Rent* sign—"

"Come *in*," the man said with sudden vivacity. "*Do.* I'm Tibor."

They agreed later that he must have stashed the sandwich in a pocket. Stepping inside, they looked around. It was a little scary. They were in a hall with niches in the walls and iron light fixtures hanging from a groined ceiling. Severe red-velvet chairs stood about. Lingering with the dankness of inactivity was another smell, pungent and unpleasant. Rosetta let Frank see her sniffing ecstatically.

"We're looking to rent a store," Frank began, and faltered.

Rosetta took over.

"We want to convert a funeral home into a comedy club called The Last Laugh, and this place is perfect."

"Why not?" said Tibor. "Used to get business from the church, and now *it's* a disco. Show you around? Foyer, of course."

"Our front bar," Rosetta said.

"Two chapels through here."

They were spacious parlors got up in scarlet beneath stained-glass windows that depicted weeping willows and tortured yews.

"Combine them, *voilà*: our showroom," said Rosetta. "Dig the windows."

After showing them the garage, Tibor took them down a staircase of shallow risers.

"This was the salesroom," he said of one bare room. "And here's the embalming room."

They entered a space that glimmered invitingly until he found the light switch. Buzzing fluorescents revealed crackled tile walls that enclosed sinks, apparatus of an unknown nature and stainless-steel tables grooved like serving platters. There were refrigerators set into the wall and wide-slotted drains on the floor.

"The *pièce de rèsistance*," said Rosetta. "Enchanting. *Love* the smell."

"Never goes away," said Tibor.

He took them into his office. An oversized book about garden furniture was open on his desk, with similar ones strewn about.

"See my thing?" he said, clearing off chairs. "Opening a store in Teaneck."

"Why did you go out of business?" Rosetta asked, sitting down. "Didn't AIDS save the day?"

"AIDS did a lot, but this isn't what I want to do with my life." Rapidly he wrote figures on black-bordered paper. "Lease runs another four years. I pay $11 a square foot, I'll sublease for $17. But he'll raise it, next lease: Forty if he can get it. Thinks the neighborhood's going places."

Seventeen dollars a square foot! They were budgeting *$30!* Rosetta and Frank looked at each other dreamily.

"Did you notice?" Rosetta asked after they left. "Everything about him screams, *'Get me out of here!'*"

"We'll do our best," said Frank.

He spent days building VisiCalc spreadsheets on his new PC. Calculating and recalculating their amber columns at a stately pace, they showed to the penny what it would cost to open The Last Laugh and how much it would bring in every quarter over five years.

It would be a gold mine.

He took pains with the Executive Summary.

"Manhattan's in a strange mood these days," he wrote,

```
as death rains down upon it. A
medieval visitation of plague has
blasted New York's freewheeling
nightlife. Sadly, AIDS promises
to be the rock and roll of the
Nineties, and while it rages
people will prefer to stay home
or, if they do venture out, will
look not for fun, but for mashed
potatoes or chicken-fried steak.
    But is comfort food the best
we can do? The Last Laugh, a
comedy club set in a former
funeral parlor, responds to the
new reality with a new concept
that acknowledges the AIDS
epidemic while fulfilling
nightlife's traditional mission
of diverting people from the
problems of the day.
```

> Established on a shrewd
> psychological basis and managed
> by an experienced team, The Last
> Laugh will scare its customers in
> the way they love to be scared,
> helping them put aside their
> fears of mortality to find joy in
> the moment.

Frank was pleased. He hoped he'd succeeded in expressing something valid that no one else was saying—in a way, updating Daniel Defoe.

He asked Conor to read it. Moaning and groaning, as a great personal concession Conor sat down and worked his way to the end.

"Good job," he said when he finished.

"Ready to show Rex?"

Smoky icicles curled out of Conor's nose.

"Just half an hour," Frank pleaded.

"OK, OK," Conor said. "How 'bout day after tomorrow, 12:00 noon? I'll fix it with Trish."

Siggy had found his replacement the day Frank gave notice.

"Man of your position needs the right voice, right face, right body. *Very* important, Rex: Don't fuck around with this.

"Happen to know a British lady name of Trish. *Perfect* secretary. Classy accent—makes the royal family sound low-rent. Ask her what her dad is, I can't keep 'em straight, earl or something. May not have money any more, but he fucking well saw to it his kid learned how to *talk*. You'll love her."

Two days later, groomed with special care (having absorbed the lesson that when asking for money one had better not look in need of any), and carrying a Velobound copy of his plan, Frank knocked at the familiar door.

A melodic English voice called "Come in!" from his old desk.

"Frank!" said Perri. "What are *you* doing here?"

"My 12:00 o'clock with Rex?"

Of whom there was no sign.

"Rex doesn't have a 12:00 o'clock," the Englishwoman volunteered.

"Conor said—"

"Wait if you want," said Perri. "I'm sure he'll be glad to see you."

Joey gave him a chair and headphones, and skimmed the plan ecstatically.

"*Killer!*" he kept saying. "Rex will *love* this!"

Rex finally stalked in.

"Fucking Morty—" he started, and froze. "Uh-oh, *here* he is! What have we in store, I'm afraid to ask?"

"Hello, Rex," said Frank. "Have an idea to share with you."

"Oh God, no avoiding your fate, is there?"

And Frank found himself settling in opposite Rex, who, gripping the armrests of his bucking chair, said, "Things to do."

Frank got down to it, telling him about Conor's inspiration and handing the business plan across. Rex riffled through it.

"The idea's to take advantage of the unconscious relation of comedy to death, and—"

"The *what* of comedy to death?"

"Unconscious relation?" Frank replied. "'Comedians explore threatening topics'—I think I'm quoting—'in order to *slay* them, to defy death with laughter. Hence, transforming a mortuary to a comedy club exploits a resonant dialectic—'"

"Frank, *honey*, what did I ever *do* to you?" Rex interrupted. "Whatever it was, I'm so *sorry!*" His eye caught a phrase. Incredulously he read it aloud: "'AIDS promises to be the rock and roll of the *Nineties'*? The *fuck?*"

"Unfortunately, AIDS is the fastest-growing—"

Rex tossed the plan back. Trish started gathering up his phone messages.

"'*Turn it into a comedy club and call it The Last Laugh*'? Hate to be the one to tell you, Frank, but Conor was *kidding*. That was a *joke*. Frankly, I wouldn't care to be *associated* with an idea like this. But best of luck."

"Thanks for listening, Rex."

Joey and Byrne waved from their phones as Frank left. At the elevator what he heard reminded him of what used to occur whenever a would-be music client dropped off a cassette. Perri always promised to listen to it, and as soon as the door closed would slip it into Joey's tapedeck, hit *Play*, give it five seconds, remark, "I've heard enough," and hit *Eject*, all before the elevator arrived.

"Believe it?" he heard Rex say. "Creeps me out. Where's the Lysol?"

Byrne said something Frank didn't catch. When the elevator carried him off, everyone was laughing.

Conor apologized for forgetting to make the appointment.

Rosetta heard Frank tell it with equanimity.

"Who wants to be partners with Rex, anyway?" she said. "Other people in this town have money."

"But who?" Frank bleated.

"Have you seen Trump Tower? Donald Trump *must* have a sense of humor. And get a copy to Felix Rohatyn. You know what would help the most? If Conor let us use his name."

She was right; however Frank touted his or her nightclub experience, it looked thin.

"No chance while he works for Rex."

"How are you two getting along, anyway?"

"Great."

"Well, your intentions are the best," Rosetta assured him. "Not that half the problems in this world can't be laid to good intentions. At *least* half."

Frank duly dropped off copies around town, always with a flash of teeth meant to flatter the receptionist. No queries resulted from this procedure, however.

"Wish I *liked* rich people," he told Rosetta. "Maybe I'd *know* some."

"It's puzzling, Frank, that's what it is. But welcome to the business we call show. Have to persevere.

"Wait, did you try D.K. Ludwig? He's a *billionaire*."

25.

BELIEF IN THE IPO vanished with Siggy. Rex felt leprous. He found meetings with prospective investors impossible to get, his phone calls refused, his notes and letters ignored. With Perri he traipsed to half a dozen banks applying for a big fat personal loan, but apparently his need communicated itself, for they shut up their cash drawers.

Nor had he any lead on Siggy, though one day he swore he saw the Daimler trundling past Carnegie Hall grimy and roadworn.

Harshaw was impatient with Rex's impatience.

"Why surface with anything federal hanging over his head? He's no idiot, Rex. Either he's living in that jalopy of his, driving around town like The Man Without a Country, or he took my advice and went to Jersey. But he'll work things out. Always does."

"For want of a fucking *nail!*" Rex wailed.

But his strength was that he could always do what had to be done.

Perri told him, "Black, if you go to Joe D., I'm leaving you. Baby and I need you *alive.*"

"*Broke?*"

"Better than *dead.*"

Made no sense to Rex. He dialed Joe D.

"Joe, so sorry to disturb you —"

"Don't tell me, no rent *again?*"

"Worse, Joe: If I don't find cash to tide us over till that fucker Siggy Brewster —"

"Ever mention he's a client of mine?"

"When he shows, we're in *clover.* But till then we're *fucked.* You're my last hope."

"How much?"

"Fifty thousand should do it, Joe. Depending. A hundred."

There was an ominous pause.

"Rex, I think you better come see me."

Heart pounding out a funeral march, his mouth dry, Rex said, "Happy to, Joe. Any time, any place."

"Come on up right now."

"On my way! . . . *Um.* Where?"

The rent check (when sent) went to a P.O. box.

"Home. Don't tell me you don't *know* — ?"

"No idea."

"Chrissakes, Rex, over your fucking *store.* Apartment 3-C."

"Joey, anything happen to me," Rex said quietly as he left, "take care of Perri and the baby, won't you?"

"Trying another bank? They won't *whack* you."

"Meeting Joe D. at long last."

That wiped the smile off Joey's face.

"Shit," he said. "Want backup?"

"Yeah, I could use some backup, but where the fuck will I find any? 'Cause I'm looking at you, Joey, and you know I love you, but —"

"All right, all right, just asking."

It was 12:00 noon when Rex walked up the steps beside the

club and found the door marked 3-C. He saw his hand rise, hesitate, knock.

Dogs barked furiously in response.

But not major dogs. Little dogs.

Yap yap yap. Yip yip yip.

"Shut up, you monsters!" roared a voice. "SHUT UP!"

But there was no letup as the door opened. Rex braced himself for a death stare from malevolence incarnate (in truth, he was also curious). He found himself dancing away from a trio of Yorkies and looking down at an old man in a wheelchair.

"COME HERE, YOU BASTARDS!"

The power of the old man's voice was surprising, given the tube running from an oxygen bottle behind the seat to his nostrils.

The dogs didn't quiet down much, but Rex found that he could ignore them, step inside, shake Joe D.'s hand and help him close the door. At the kitchen table he took the chair indicated.

"Having lunch," Joe D. grunted. "Hungry?"

"No, that's all right," said Rex. Bologna with dark curled edges sat on slices of bread on a cracked plate. "You go ahead."

As Joe D. noisily coaxed mustard from an empty bottle, Rex glanced around. It was a nightmare of an old man's place, messy and smelly, especially from newspapers lining the floor for the dogs' benefit. Detecting a cleaner tang, too, he traced it to a counter where barber's tools were neatly laid out: clippers, scissors, combs soaking in alcohol, bottles of hair oil and bay rum, a lethal array of straight razors.

"OK, Rex. Say what you came to say."

While Rex poured out his tale of woe—a woe so easily retrievable with a negligible, absolutely *final* cash infusion—

Joe D. shoved a sandwich in his mouth. Crumbs sprinkled lap and floor and the smudged floral oilcloth as he chewed. Yorkies snapped.

"Won't get money out of *me*," he said. "This crummy firetrap's all I got in the world, and it's breaking down even faster'n I am. Wasted your trip."

He slapped a fly.

"Have to pay your rent, Rex," he went on, wiping his hand on the oilcloth. "What I don't understand is why Siggy hasn't called you."

"He's *back?*"

"Came by for a shave and a haircut the other day. Has a new place in the West 50s. Very solid setup, he tells me."

He turned and dialed a mustard-yellow wall phone.

"'Lo, it's Joe D.," he spoke into it with Darth Vader gasps. Then, "Siggy! *Schmuck*, why haven't you called Rex Black? Says unless—" He listened for a moment, handed the receiver to Rex and greedily began pinching up crumbs from his lap.

Siggy apologized fulsomely to Rex, said he'd been about to call, having updated everything with the SEC so that his new firm, The Cromwell Companies, could take over the IPO from Maple Tree Investors.

"Great firm," Siggy said. "Old school. We're in your neighborhood, feel at home already. Come for lunch tomorrow, we'll decide when we should *go.*"

Joe D. waved off Rex's thanks at the door.

"Hell, cut his hair from a kid, can't take my phone calls?"

Back at the office Rex said, "Teaches you about facing your fears."

"How was it?" asked Joey.

"Joey, it's *over*, that's all that matters, I did it, and I'm in one piece."

"Thank God, Black," said Perri. "Thank *God*."

Rex nodded curtly.

"Was Germano right about him?" Joey asked.

"My gut churned—can't help it, look into those eyes, you see he's cut a hundred throats in his day. But unlike Germano I did *not* shit my pants, and I hope you tell him so."

Perri said, "I'm only surprised you'd do business with *Siggy*, after he left us in the lurch."

"I'm a practical person," Rex explained.

Next day he found the address: A grand limestone townhouse off Fifth Avenue. Beside the door a shiny brass plate identified The Cromwell Companies. Bore holes dripped calcified green where other signs used to hang.

Standing in the crosshairs of surveillance cameras, Rex rang. The glass and wrought-iron door opened and seven feet of ebony confronted him, eyes passing rapidly over his person.

"Appointment, sir?"

"Rex Black? Mr. Brewster's expecting me?"

Another man made a quiet call from beside an inner door, and moments later Noah Winsocket shambled in, brushing aside his shock of hair.

"Welcome, Mr. Black," he said.

"Thanks, Noah." Happily Rex murmured, "Like trying to get on fucking El Al. They carry?"

"Surely," said Noah, taking him past gilded pilasters into a chamber whose Waterford chandelier splashed light across blue-and-silver Chinese export paper.

Siggy bumbled in, Noah receding, and kissed Rex on the cheek.

"Rex! What you think? Like a museum, am I right?"

"Beautiful."

They sat down. Rex almost slipped off his chair's silken upholstery as he craned at gilt vitrines displaying collections of ivory and coral *netsuke*. Over the mantelpiece hung a portrait of a man whose aureole of white hair shone against a burgundy background.

"Landed on your feet," he remarked. "So, Siggy, what *happened?* Where you *been?*"

They smiled at each other.

"I think you're confused," said Siggy. "We were Downtown, then we moved up here. Finally got religion, Midtown's where it's at. Don't tell me Barbie forgot the change-of-*address* card? She ever going to get it!

"Fine old firm," he added. "That's Old Man Cromwell over the fireplace. Financed utilities in the Twenties. Great man. Man of honor. Died in Leavenworth, but they never got a word out of him."

Siggy communed contentedly with the old man's inflamed red eyes.

Over steaks on TV trays, Rex urged, *"When, Siggy? When?"*

"Soon," Siggy purred. "As a matter, how does Thursday sound? Market's right and my gut says *'Go!'* Come on by, watch it happen."

26.

ON IPO DAY, REX took Joey and Byrne with him to haul freebies for the bankers and brokers.

Joey and Byrne didn't get past the lobby. Instead, Noah Winsocket helped Rex carry the cartons—via a second-floor bridge—to Cromwell's trading floor in the adjacent tower of polished pink granite, a room that resembled NASA Mission Control. Flashing screens lighted the faces of men and women dewy of eye, with hair fresh from the attentions of blow dryer and gel bottle.

Curiously, the women's voices tended to be deeper than the men's; the men chirped their concern at the Yankees while the women growled about the Quotron.

Siggy waved from the corner where he was conferring with what looked like some shady types, but everybody else crowded around as, crouching, Rex lifted out sweatshirts and baseball caps stitched with the Gag Reflex logo and *IPO 1987*. Everyone pulled on a sweatshirt, clapped on a hat and went back to work.

Rex felt like the best man at a wedding, in the middle of things but peripheral. He was standing at a loss when Siggy, having finally accepted a cap, had Noah shunt him to a waiting room well supplied with golf magazines.

"Not much to see yet," Noah explained.

Rex used the phone in the corner to wake up Conor.

"Conor, getting my money today, and you're going out to L.A. and open up a new Gag Reflex *chop chop.*"

"What about the one here?"

"Sly can take care of it." Sly had been assistant manager for several months. "Runs itself, you got things going so smooth. And you have your raise: What am I paying you, 600? How's *750* sound?"

"Rex—"

"There a problem?"

"You *promised* to renovate after the IPO."

"Good," said Rex. "*Great.* Only I got bigger fish to fry. Fucking *beer* box? I promised before certain facts of life bit me in the ass, one of them being that club's magic *because* it's a shithole! Look, open L.A. and we'll talk."

"OK, Rex, OK. You win."

"How will the boyfriend be with your going out of town?"

"Fine."

"Trish'll do your ticket and hotel."

Greatest day of Rex's life, but he was not in the best of moods. He called the office to lambaste Joey.

"Needed Racquel's record out *before* the IPO, and even now, they're still *mixing?*"

"They're close, Rex," said Joey. "*Very* close."

"Do we at least have a Number One record?"

"C'mon, no one ever knows—"

"Your *job* is on the line, Joey."

"Top Forty, I swear. Probably Top *Ten*, and just *maybe*—"

"Put Perri on."

"Black!" said Perri. "How's it going? Are we public?"

"Happening as we speak," he told her. "The electrons are zipping. Just awesome."

He heard her say, "Yeah, we're public," and Joey shout, "*Yippee*-IPO! *Yippee*-IPO!"

"So proud of you," Perri told him. "Must be so happy."

"How are *you*? Feeling better?"

She'd arisen not feeling her best. Rex urged her to stay home, but she insisted on working right up to delivery.

"Not so great," she admitted. "Think I'm about to get out of here."

"Good idea," said Rex. "Get some rest."

He hung up and studied golf swings.

"*Rex!* Wondered where the fuck you got to!" Siggy called from the doorway. "Come see the action."

He pulled Rex through unsettling streams of lighted numbers crawling and blinking to every side while backwards baseball caps hit keys or barked on phones (baseball caps were worn in rally position after Mets fans' turning them that way won Game Six of the 1986 World Series). Behind glass Rex saw men in sweaters tending a mainframe computer like priests at the altar.

"Are we public yet?" he asked. No one answered. Kids punched keys ferociously. "Are we public?"

"Yeah, it's soup," Siggy said. "Put it on the zipper. Rex, congratulations!"

Bright red letters began growling NASDAQ trades: *GRX 4 7/8 . . . GRX 4 13/16 . . . GRX 4 2/3 . . .*

A waiter poured champagne. Rex knew it was joy he felt — *his dream realized!* — but also he wondered, *Is this all there is?*

"So what's the price?"

"What'd I tell you? Almost every share's going to sell, average maybe 4.65."

"I thought *five*? Or more?"

"Five," said Siggy, as though it were an explanation.

"But it's heading *down?*"

"Goes up, means we left money on the table. Not my style. Won't fall much."

"Siggy, I love you," said Rex. "Made me rich today. Knock off, let me take you out."

"Love to, Rex, only see those guys? Sincerely wish I could, but they're going public next week, deal worth 20 million. Coming thing, cellular phones."

"Know the way it goes, guys," Rex called over. His deal aggregated some $4 million. "But in the end it's worth it."

"Thanks, Rex, thank you very much," said Siggy, whose finger-snap called up Noah Winsocket. "Money's on the wire to your bank. See you very soon."

Noah escorted Rex out.

"What a fuck," Rex muttered as he walked back to the office. "Suddenly I'm yesterday's doughnuts? *Cell* phones? Fucking bottom feeder."

He kicked at a pigeon and entered the office seething. He found only Byrne.

"Fuck *is* everybody?"

"Mt. Sinai," said Byrne, covering the receiver. "Perri just had the baby. Nine pounds, two ounces. Joey's with her, everything's fine."

"The fuck, *without* me? Had it *without* me?" That took him to his desk. "Dammit, things to *do!* But I better get up there."

He left.

When Perri hung up with Rex she said, "Joey, this is it. Get a cab, please."

She used the bathroom and carried downstairs the suitcase that had stalked her for weeks past. At Mt. Sinai Joey coached her through the birth of her daughter (but then, he'd gotten to more Lamaze classes than Rex had).

Rex had chosen the name Sarah. Perri named her child Clarissa. If she started her pregnancy with the sense of becoming mother to all the world's children, she ended it the mother of a specific willful charmer 17 inches long.

27.

REX'S TURNING DOWN The Last Laugh ruined it for Frank because it extinguished Conor's interest in it — or shoved in his face the fact that Conor *had* no interest in it. For a short while he continued to distribute the business plan. Responses were limited to an amused few asking if anyone else was investing.

Then he gave it up and looked for work.

"If it somehow comes alive, fine, I'm on the job," he told Rosetta. "If Donald Trump writes us a check, for instance."

"Good," she said.

The job Frank got was proofreading Saturday and Sunday nights at a white-shoe Wall Street law firm. It paid the rent and gave him the week for taking a fresh look at *Foe*, and his colleagues were an interesting bunch, so it wasn't a bad deal.

During Conor's absence in L.A., Frank stayed at his own place, but went by Bleecker Street most days to pick up the mail. The round trip made for a good walk.

One hot August evening he walked rapidly down Sixth Avenue on that errand. At the corner of 23rd Street he found himself standing amidst one of the decade's common sights in New York, where was exploded onto the public way a short lifetime's quantum of *stuff*: record albums, books, knick-knacks, porn (invariably gay), shirts as carelessly dropped, pants as intimately crooked, as on a bedroom floor. Conor would have gone through everything with serious mien and salvaged an armload; Frank continued on his way.

That *memento mori* perfectly complemented the neighborhood he entered south of 23rd, with its sense of life departed amidst monuments of a bygone age. He chose his route so as to pass the *For Rent* sign rotting in the funeral parlor's window. If The Last Laugh was the tomb of certain hopes he had relating to Conor, still he liked seeing the sign.

But tonight it was gone, and the sidewalk in front was trampled with plaster dust. Bare bulbs glared indoors. Sheets of plywood secured by chains replaced the front doors, and dumpsters hulked in the street.

Frank called Rosetta from the next corner.

"Rosetta, guess what: They're renovating our funeral home!"

"No shit!"

"No clue who took it. I'll go by during the day and try to find out."

"*Do.* But it's not the only funeral parlor in town, Frank."

"No, but it was *perfect. Dammit!* Oh well, it was fun while it lasted."

"I'm glad you feel that way. Me, too."

Next afternoon Frank found a crew wheeling out smashed plaster.

"Excuse me," he asked. "Can you please tell me who's rented this space?"

"Won't believe it," answered a grinning workman. "Comedy club with a funeral-home theme. Best part? Guess what it's called."

"The Last Laugh?" Frank ventured.

The man's mouth went sour. He spat.

"Yep."

Frank waited until he got home to call Rosetta.

"Hey, Rosetta."

"Hey, Frank."

"Rosetta, I went by the funeral home again and got the lowdown."

"*And?*"

"It's going to be a comedy club. Called The Last Laugh."

"You're *shitting* me!"

"Quite a coincidence," Frank offered.

"In New York you can *count* on coincidence," Rosetta said. "Just as you can count on *life* to be *funny* . . . Hullo? *Hullo?*"

"Rosetta, what's going on?"

"Well, Siggy Brewster found the money, and I know you don't want anything to do with *that* crowd."

"Rosetta, before you ever *heard* of The Last Laugh, I−"

She hung up.

Frank dialed, listened to six rings, and wrote a letter:

```
Dear Rosetta,

    The Last Laugh is a joint
project of yours and mine and
Conor Brennan's. Conor conceived
the idea, and you and I marketed
it using the business plan I
wrote with your input.

    If you pursue The Last Laugh
without Conor's participation or
mine, I will take legal action
against you—but, Rosetta, aren't
we friends as well as partners?
```

He put a regular stamp on it, resisting a legalistic impulse to send it certified mail, return receipt requested.

A few days later an envelope with no return address arrived. He opened it to find his letter smeared with feces, with an addition in round red characters:

> *thanks for writing I needed toilet*
> *paper so sue me faggot!! go ahead!!*

"Let it go, Dolls," Conor advised from California. "Cunt from day one."

"*You* brought her in."

"But if *she* dug up the money . . ."

"Yeah?"

"It's her idea now."

Rosetta went to Siggy the day after Rex's IPO. Gaining entry to The Cromwell Companies wasn't easy; she had to hold up an archive of headshots to the cameras before seven feet of ebony cracked the door, then wait for Barbie to show her in to the presence.

"Miss Rosetta Stone!" exclaimed Siggy when at last she entered. "How nice to see you. Oh, did you make me laugh that night! I still ache! And what can I do for *you*?"

"Rex didn't think I was so funny," Rosetta reminded him.

"Rex has no sense of humor. Somebody laughs, he checks his fly. Bad sign for someone in the comedy business."

She handed him The Last Laugh business plan, Frank's name effaced from it.

"This is a new concept in nightclubs, one just right for today," she said. "Comedy club-slash-disco in a funeral home, and I've got the perfect space, *cheap*."

"Still kicking myself about the Hard Rock," said Siggy. "Rex see this?"

"Turned it down."

Paging through it, he asked, "You really blow him?"

"I'm very oral."

They reached an agreement quite soon thereafter.

To expedite the liquor licensing, a bore Siggy preferred to avoid, Rosetta would be the owner of record. Naturally, she would also perform as headliner-in-residence.

It was fun, having the last laugh.

28.

REX CONCENTRATED on getting Raquel's record out.

Late September was good timing, he hoped, when night falls surprisingly early, giving people a daily sense of dislocation, and sound travels its mysterious extra autumn distance: Something new might stand a chance. He decreed that the release of album, single and video be marked with a party at the club that Joey dubbed *Bash for the Smash.*

"Call in your markers," Rex commanded him, "if you have any. If *What You Do To Me* sells, it jacks up the stock. Misses, I can pack it in."

"Me, too," ventured Joey.

"Won't have to, I'll do it for you."

Meanwhile Perri, eschewing a nanny, set up a bassinet beside her desk, a crib in the conference room and brought Clarissa to work with her. She cleared the last New Age artifacts out of her life, passing them on to Ashley, and attacked the accumulated bills with what Rex told her was unseemly gusto.

"Go easy," he cautioned. "Didn't get rich so I could pay my fucking *bills.*"

But bills had to be paid, and the money that in prospect seemed a Golconda began to melt away without much to show for it. Expenses were enormous, given Rex's feeling that his little firm had to make its presence *felt*. New clients were signed, on their behalf numerous trips taken (first class all the way), myriad costly meals fed to grizzled veterans of the Biz. And space for new clubs was expensively secured and managers recruited, not only in Los Angeles but in Boston, Chicago and Las Vegas.

Rex expanded his office staff, too. Renting a room down the hall, he stuffed in two new hires: He stole Chester, his accountant, away from his firm, and Chester brought his assistant and her computer. She sat dabbing at its keyboard all day; no one else knew how to run it, and she wasn't telling.

But not even the excitements of the IPO could stanch the saga of Ashley's roommate and her boyfriend. Ashley told Perri that Dickhead's wife had dropped the kid.

"She *had* it?" Perri said from the depths of calm and strength that was the gift of her motherhood. "Owns him now."

"You think? He can't stand her. She gained like 200 pounds."

Self-conscious about the maternal grandeur clinging to her own body, Perri said uncomfortably, "You're exaggerating."

"Not in his eyes."

"Well, your roommate's never going to get him, not unless she comes down with a disease-of-the-week or something. And Ashley, I know she's a friend of yours, but she *sounds* — "

"No friend of *mine*, Perri. I *hate* the bitch."

"But you know what? I feel sorry for her."

"You would," Ashley said under her breath.

Bash for the Smash? Joey saw to everything. He personally dropped off CD and single at every radio station in town, and delivered the video to MTV, VH-1 and *Friday Night Videos* with strict injunctions against playing it before Friday midnight (Rex was delighted when the embargo held). Also he procured a suite for Racquel at the Mayflower Hotel.

The evening of the *Bash* was balmy and benevolent. Ginger's new superstretch dropped off Rex and Perri, he in black tie, she in the slinkiest outfit she'd dared in a year. With gawky unease Rex extended his arm, and together they maneuvered through the moguls gathered on the sidewalk. But their welcome couldn't have been warmer; Racquel's songs wafting overhead, moguls hugged them mercilessly.

Inside, where space was cleared for a buffet and dancing, and where the video—Racquel soulfully wringing her hands against a brick wall with her skirt hiked up—looped endlessly on big-screen TVs, Rex found more smiles, more embraces. Industry *crème de la crème* milled, happy to be drinking him dry. Rex had personally invited every enemy and every friend he had in the music business.

Even Germano made an appearance. "Glad Tinny came through for you," he told Rex, before asking what he'd done to the club's old magic.

Darting at Rex's ear, prodding his back, pulling at his wrists, everybody confided that they *loved* the album, the single, the video, Racquel, *him*.

"So much there!" they shouted.

"It's *packed*," Rex yelled back.

He enjoyed heartwarming chats with Clive, Ahmet, Lou, with George and Tommy and Jimmy, hugged Jellybean, touched glasses with Paul. Janos he kissed while suits from the label described the unparalleled support they were throwing behind the CD.

Racquel and Joey arrived waving out the sunroof of the superstretch. Racquel flew about, never alighting, a tiny, excited, long-limbed person who refreshed every table she visited. Persuaded to perform impromptu (after four rehearsals with the house band), she stopped her CD and sang live in a thinner but affecting voice.

As she sang *What You Do To Me* Rex looked around her enraptured audience and had veritably an out-of-body experience, seeing himself at the center of a web of love and fame and money. Around him the hardest characters in the toughest business he knew were surreptitiously rubbing away the tears this delicate girl called forth just with her breath.

Clive whispered, "Big talent."

"Move over, Madonna," thought Rex. "New girl's in town!"

Joey danced with whoops of joy and liberal spills of tequila deep into the night.

Rex had been around long enough to know to go by Tower Records first thing in the morning, see with his own eyes the product walking out of the store in the hands of actual customers. Beat waiting for the hard numbers in the following week's *Billboard*.

Tingling with anticipation, wide awake despite having slept only a couple of hours, he cabbed down to the Village early, when the streets were empty and fast. If kids were camped out in front he'd spring for—*what?* Pizza? No, hot chocolate! And doughnuts! When the store opened he'd check the displays, count the units, make sure they were restocked as necessary. How early did he dare wake up Racquel with the good news?

But no kids encumbered the sidewalk outside Tower Records, and when the doors opened Rex was the only person waiting. He strolled around inside, made his findings, left, found a phone—in an actual red-paneled booth reeking of urine—and woke Joey up from a Technicolor dream.

"Joey, little problem!" he said. "Just left Tower Records. Went in to buy a copy of Racquel's CD, you know? So glad I did: What a *bargain!*"

"What do you mean?"

"I mean if you go in and bear left, you'll find a thing on wheels made for *garbage,* and piled in it every copy they've got of her album — CD *and* cassette — priced at two bucks, 'cause that's their $2 junk pile, I mean bargain bin.

"Two dollars, Joey: Your fucking record just went double *plutonium!"*

"Rex, they don't know —"

"But they *do,* Joey. Selling records is their *business.* They can tell what's hot from last year's model."

"It's a slap at Janos —"

"It's not that asshole, it's *business,*" Rex explained patiently. "They get the product in, give a listen and if it's shit, into the toilet it goes. Now, if we'd given 'em a *hit* record — While you were at it, why not make a *hit* record?"

"You said you loved it. I think it's beautiful."

"How can it be beautiful if it's in the diaper pail?" Rex asked. "Two *dollars?* Hope you like your stock options under water, Joey, 'cause they're *drowning!*"

When Joey slipped into the office Monday morning, Rex shoved his door open and spoke in cold anger across Trish and Perri and Byrne.

"Joey, do me a favor, call up Racquel, remind her she owes me whatever it is — for recording, *et cetera.* Her lease car. Janos. And so on. It's in the folder. One twenty, ballpark."

$120,000.

"She doesn't have that kind of money!"

"Maybe she's ahead in her checking account or something. After taking *me* for everything I've *got.*" Rex advanced into the bullpen. *"Shit!* Try doing something, and know what happens?

People *want* you to fail. No reason they should care one way or the other, but if it's the same to you, they prefer that you *fail*, thank you very much. People in this town are cannibals." He turned, stared out the window. "Must be fucking dreaming. I can look outdoors and remember there's so much out of life to get! But the $2 bargain bin! Not to mention The Come-Ons walking."

"We couldn't get them a record deal," Joey reminded him.

"Not even a high-school band from Podunk USA wants *you* to manage 'em. I love you, Joey —"

"Love *you*, Rex."

" — but I can't afford your mistakes. As CEO of a public company I have to answer to my stockholders. You're *fired*."

"Black!" cried Perri.

"Rex, no!" cried Trish and Byrne.

Rex looked pleased with himself, bemused at his own ruthlessness.

"That's all right," Joey assured his colleagues. "He can't fire *me*: I *quit!*"

"Fuck you!" said Rex.

"Fuck you!" said Joey.

"Fuck you!"

"Fuck you!"

"Fuck you!"

"Stop it, Joey," Perri screamed. *"Stop* it!"

"Look what you've done! Made Perri cry! Get out! Off the premises before I call security!"

Joey left.

Rex called Siggy to see if Wall Street liked Raquel's album any better than Tower Records did.

While the stock market surged to record heights that summer — the Dow Jones Industrial Average reached a heady peak of 2,722 on August 25 — malign fates gathered over the price of Gag Reflex, Inc. and it settled as though it had a leak.

Rex's plan had been for shares to hit the market at $5, double the first day and march upwards to $15, $20, $25 and beyond to the *boom! boom! boom!* of Raquel's hit record, The Come-Ons sensation and the landmark new club in L.A.

Instead, the stock never quite touched $5 before it commenced sinking — to $4, $3.50, $2.75, $2.25, $1.75, $1.25. After an extended flirtation with $1, it began swooning through every dreary fraction of the stock tables. Security analysts described the Gag Reflex client roster as *iffy* and said the New York club was due an expensive renovation and — most ominous of all — that the stand-up comedy boom was peaking in popularity.

"Siggy, 50 *cents?*" Rex now complained.

"Rex, way it goes. That's the market for you. Who says it's rational?"

Rex mentioned a *Short Interest Report* in the *Times* that listed his among the companies some were selling short.

Siggy meant to be reassuring.

"Only sophisticated investors play that game, Rex, and win or lose, they never make a fuss."

"But betting *against* me? Going to lose their shirts, right?"

"Now, did I say that? Please don't put words in my mouth. Credibility is all anyone's got in this business."

"Siggy, *you're* not short —?"

"Wouldn't know. Think I handle my portfolio? Could be at that, my guy hates exposure, offsets everything. 'Seymour,' I tell him, 'lighten up, have some *fun.*' Seymour looks at me like I'm nuts. Have to let you go, Rex: Got to take this call."

Of course, Rex relented and Joey was back in his employ by the end of the week.

But he was a changed Joey. His passage struck off speed lines no longer; rather, he agglomerated his way along the walls. Soon Rex was joking that he knew Joey was there only when he noticed something blocking the light.

What happened could happen to anyone. Late the night he was fired—*quit*—as he and Phil, his lover, were entwined in bed, gloomily watching HBO, Joey sneezed. It came with his back in a funny position. Pain shot through his spine.

"Joey, what *happened?*" Perri asked as he limped through the bullpen his first day back at work.

Joey's pain was growing into an entity he'd never conceived of, an insistent red pool that blotted everything else from consciousness.

"Threw out my back or something," he explained. "From all the backstabbing."

29.

WHEN REX GOT TO THE OFFICE on the morning of Monday, October 19, 1987, the New York Stock Exchange had been crashing as hard and fast as it could for half an hour.

It continued in freefall for the rest of the day. The Dow Jones Industrial Average lost 508 points, more than 22% — its worst one-day drop *ever*, prevented from going even lower only by such spontaneous NYSE measures as shutting down for several breathers and closing early. The Amex and NASDAQ followed. Gag Reflex opened at 3/8 asked, 1/4 bid. It closed at a price denominated in 32nds of a dollar.

The market's collapse was unnerving to sit through. Everybody in Rex's office was quiet, preoccupied and none too efficient. Chester made a few white-faced appearances from down the hall.

Rex doggedly tried to ignore events on Wall Street and tend to business. He hunted for a paying gig for Hank Washburn. The previous Friday Hank had finally been booked on *Letterman* — oh, the labors it had taken! Ashley accompanied him to the green room to keep him sober, but unfortunately Maria Conchita Alonso went long and Hank got bumped.

Rex was livid. This was supposed to be the week when, fresh off a triumphant *Letterman* shot, he approached Carson's people. Instead he was looking for a bread-and-butter job, and doing it as a favor since Hank was between agents.

Half a dozen phone calls later, he finally came up with a Cleveland burglar-alarm convention that wanted a comedian to address it in the guise of a reformed smash-and-grab artist. At least it was something.

Over the phone Hank expressed gratitude to Rex, then asked Trish to exchange the first-class airline ticket the convention was providing for one in economy, and to refund the difference to him in cash. Trish spent two hours at that intricate task. When Rex found out, he went ballistic.

"Let's cut him loose! *Today!* Letterman knows, Hank's TV *poison*. Book him at all the conventions we like, commissions won't even keep Clarissa in Pampers!"

Rex yelled at Hank over the phone, told him he was tearing up his contract, and did it, jamming the receiver close to capture the sound of ripping paper. It made the bullpen an even more uncomfortable place. Trish took a long lunch. Byrne went shopping.

Meanwhile Joey listened to the radio's monotonous *down down down down down* stretched flat on the floor.

"Hasn't complained once about his back," Perri said *sotto voce* to Ashley.

"Stock market crash? Better than Percodan."

Finally, in late afternoon, Rex stalked out to the bullpen.

"What's this, my little collection of lost souls fiddling while Rome burns? Shit, what a day."

"What's it doing?" asked Perri.

"Sky's falling in. Dow's down—"

"I mean Gag Reflex."

"Don't want to know. Off the map. Fucking atomic hit."

"What'll we do?" she asked.

"Go to Plan B," Rex answered.

"What's Plan B?"

"Working on it." He bared his teeth to show he'd made a joke. "One thing to remember: Entertainment's recession-proof. The Great Depression *made* Hollywood. This could be *our* chance."

It didn't fly. He stalked back to his office and stood at the window, scanning nearby buildings to see if anybody was jumping. No one was, but others were also standing at their windows looking out.

Perri asked Ashley the latest about her roommate.

"Still with Dickhead, but who knows what's going to happen now that he's *broke.*"

"His *company's* gone?"

"After today—"

"If the wife's smart, she'll end up with it. New York's not a community property state, but—"

"But if nothing's left?"

"There's *always* something left. Give her Siggy's number."

Ashley looked at her coolly. Perri returned to her work.

Finally—it was Rex's idea—they got Ginger's superstretch and (except for Perri, who took Clarissa home) went off for a roaring drunken dinner, followed by a raucous evening at the club, which Rex was ecstatic to find packed to the rafters despite its being Open Mic Monday, slowest night of the week.

Frank had gotten home that morning from his Sunday night shift around 9:00 a.m., and consequently slept through the Crash unawares. The answering machine woke him up in late afternoon.

"Dolls? Pick up if—"

"Conor!"

"*Hey*-ya, Dolls." Conor's voice seemed warmer over long

distance than when he was in the same room. "What a thing, huh?"

"What's that?"

"The Crash. Stock market crash?"

"Oh no, what – ?"

"End of civilization as we know it, or something. Dolls, just talked to Rex. Told him I have to see you – spousal visitation, like in prison. If you could get time off work and spring for airfare, you can share my hotel room. How 'bout it?"

"Sure!"

"Not that we'll see much of each other. Wouldn't believe what comes up, opening a nightclub."

"My consolation is Rosetta may be finding that out for herself," Frank said.

So he embarked for the Film Forum on Houston Street groggy but happy (his Monday routine being to sleep, stagger to a movie, go back to bed and wake up Tuesday morning back on a daytime schedule).

New York that night was a jangled, fractured world whose pretended hilarity harmonized with its candy-colored skyline. Carousal rang out from the Irish bars of Ninth Avenue, the Black bars of the West 40s and the gay bars of Chelsea, including one Frank could never pass without getting hard looks from beneath patent-leather visors.

Tonight something in the sight of him walking past brought people outdoors shouting at him more than once. He preferred not to make out their exact words, but proceeded watchfully. Certain seams of Manhattan Island were springing leaks. To every side sirens wailed.

From 23rd Street he headed down Sixth Avenue to check on The Last Laugh's construction. At first work appeared to go fast, but then to stall, giving Frank the unkind but pleasing thought that the project was becoming Rosetta's folly and money pit.

The neighborhood's sense of desertion suited the day, but from blocks away he could see an oasis blazing forth: The Altar. People thronged its railings like a crowd in a movie come to the cathedral for reassurance.

But coming around the corner he was astonished to find an even bigger crowd outside The Last Laugh. Resplendent and alive with lights, its façade was surmounted by a grinning neon Reaper whose scythe cut in rapid jerks. A man with a nose ring culled the mob from atop a milk carton, nodding some inside but sending many more scurrying humiliated away. Seeing Frank, he magisterially extended an arm and parted the crowd while minions unhooked the velvet rope.

"Why not?" thought Frank.

Going inside, joining what seemed the giddiest wake ever, he examined the changes made since his tour. It had been redone cheaply—woodwork spray-painted gold, for instance. Still, it had its effect, and young trendies wandered with glazed eyes.

Suddenly Rosetta shrieked a greeting. She hugged him, kissed him, yanked him to a bar made of varnished coffin lids.

"Frank! We open Friday, and now *this*: The stock market crashes! What *luck!* Isn't it *fantastic?*"

He studied her as she turned aside to order and instruct and greet and scream. She looked different but terrific, dolled up in a dress of tongue-in-cheek flamboyance—Bob Mackie, maybe?

"A dream come true," he agreed.

"Should check out the embalming room, won't believe it! Great seeing you, Frank, but have to run: 9:00 o'clock show. Sold out, I'm afraid! But you're on our list. Al," she told a hovering bouncer, "take care of him, won't you? He's on the list. Wish me luck!"

Smiling, she left him. Before Frank could turn to Al, hands propelled him down the bar, through a door, down a funereal passageway and—with a shove—halfway across the garage. Falling hard on hands and knees, he rasped his palms with grit and stopped a drug deal in the corner cold. Brushing himself off, he found holes in his pants knees.

"Hey, at least you rate the VIP door," said Al, adding, "*Scumbag.*"

30.

THE NEXT DAY, Rex headed out of the office at noon.

Perri looked up as he was leaving.

"Where you off to, Black?"

"Life goes on, Perri," he growled. "Lunch at the Odeon with the Casimir Agency about Hank. Ashley's meeting us."

Of course he made up with Hank. Rex himself Scotch-taped their contract back together. Hank's lawyer told him he'd better.

Perri ordered in and ate while she drafted a press release for the opening of the L.A. club, expected soon, with one ear to the radio's happy news that stocks were up.

Byrne transferred a call to her.

"Hello?" she said into the maw of a P.A. system echoing in her ear. *"Hello?"*

Finally she could just make out Rex speaking: " — need you to pour oil on the waters with Casimir, Trish, but not one fucking *word* to Perri, got that?"

"Black? This *is* Perri."

"The fuck's *Trish?*"

"Lunch, Black. I answer her line when she's at lunch. What

is it? What's that *noise?"*

"I'm at New York Cornell," he said. "Emergency room."

Perri's heart thudded.

"Are you all right?"

"It's Ashley. Cerebral event, they're with her now. Dropped like a rock, I fucking saved her *life!* CPR, the whole *schmear."*

"My God, Black! Poor Ashley!"

"Look, reason I'm calling—"

"New York *Cornell?"*

"Closest E.R."

"To the *Odeon?"*

"No, her *apartment."*

Perri saw that boulder from *Indiana Jones and The Raiders of the Lost Ark* rolling at her. She couldn't evade it. Trembling, she asked, "Black, what were you doing in Ashley's *apartment?"*

"Hanging *curtains,* the fuck you think? Look, tell Trish she needs to—"

"Was her roommate home?"

"What roommate?"

What Perri couldn't abide was the look of woe Joey was giving her.

Rex at the odd noise in Ashley's bedroom turned around to find her on the floor, eyes open and crazy with pain. That got him going: 911, then CPR when he found she wasn't breathing and the light was fading from her eyes.

"Need Trish to reschedule Casimir, also double-check they got Hank's promo kit. Got that?"

"But you lied about lunch!"

"But I do have a 3:00 o'clock with them which I am *not* the fuck going to *make."*

"OK, Black," she said. "See you when we see you, I guess."

She hung up. Hung up and stared at the phone.

Byrne was so struck he put his own call on hold.

"Perri, what's the matter?"

"It's Black," she said, then came to herself. She lifted Clarissa, mewing, from her bassinet. "I mean Ashley. She's in the hospital."

Before anyone could say anything she went into Rex's office, closed the door and sat down at his desk. She could see a beefy man in a Carnegie Hall studio open his mouth and let go in utter silence. At an earlier stage of her life, she might have started throwing things, acting out, confident someone would intervene before she actually climbed out a window. But she was on her own now — on her own, and her own life secondary to her child's.

Giving her breast to Clarissa, Perri dialed Siggy Brewster on Rex's private line.

At first Siggy was wary.

"Not calling about the stock price, are you? Out of my hands."

"Need your help, Siggy. I'm divorcing Black. I'll come out with half his shares — they're in my name already — and I want you to help me take the Gag Reflex private again."

Hearing his intake of breath — and mistaking his admiration for concern — she rushed to explain.

"Stock's in the gutter, it'll cost next to nothing, and if we let go the *dreams*, concentrate on the *club* — "

"Mind made up, do what I can," said Siggy. "Only cloud on the horizon's friend Harshaw's bill."

"I forgot!"

"Rex hasn't, trust me. He knows if he can't pay it, Harshaw could put him into Chapter 11. Which come to think of it — Leave Harshaw to me."

"And does the SEC need to know?"

"I'll take care of everything, Perri. Your job's to look after your precious baby."

"So we've got a deal, Siggy?"

"Yes, we do," he answered. "Always said you were the brains of the outfit. Ask Rex if you don't believe me — but not now: Mum's the word."

Joey came in and hugged her.

"I'll make sure he marries her," she assured him. "They make the perfect couple." She pulled herself up short. "God, what an evil thing to say."

31.

THE PLANE A FEW DAYS LATER—tanned people yammering in casual undress—seemed already California, not that Frank had ever been. He glued his face to the window, until severe glances from those around him gave rise to a flight attendant's edict, and he obediently pulled down the shade to facilitate the viewing of *Dirty Dancing*.

The shade closed on the deep-dyed, if autumnal, vegetation of the East and opened two hours later on the West's bare geology. The plane found the basin scooped from scratchy hills, looped the downtown spires and dropped into LAX.

Frank headed for Conor's hotel in a taxi. Neighborhoods of faded pastel passed beneath the freeway. His first impression was of flimsiness and disorder—bodyshops, office buildings, houses, drive-ins all jammed together. The prevalence of bashed-in fenders surprised him. Broad stains the color of excrement painted the center of every lane. On the other side a panicked dog ran against traffic, but the cab went forward before he could see what happened. Los Angeles struck him as less a city than a suburb grotesquely swelling out of a suburb's youthful figure, its unifying element the cracked and misaligned pavement.

They slid off the freeway onto a street lined on both sides with palm trees that resembled graphic expressions of ack-ack fire: *Pom! Pom! Pom!* Shadows splattered stucco walls.

Nosing uphill, the taxi arrived at La Mirada. Frank ducked out under extravagantly broad leaves and dodged a Bentley picking up a crone in wig and slacks — a woman perhaps to her own eyes unchanged from her pre-War prime. He got a key to Conor's room, stashed his suitcase and walked down the Sunset Strip eager to find his lover.

A giant Gag Reflex sign was up, dark but looming as though at the flip of a switch it would regurgitate the entire scene. The building's windows still sported busty pink silhouettes from its former incarnation ("Not another strip joint!" Rex exclaimed. "Three syllables," Conor explained. *"Location"*).

Hammering resounded from inside the open doors. Paint fumes stung him as he went inside.

"*Hey*-ya, Dolls."

"Conor!"

Conor crushed him in his embrace.

"Dolls, this is André, this is José," he said, his arms still claiming Frank. "They're painting the place. You know I always say a coat of paint covers a multitude of sins."

He showed him around. It was far roomier than the New York club, and generations newer. Things were in the maximum uproar of applying the finishing touches. He claimed to have the magic halfway installed.

Though Conor urged him to catch a movie, Frank contented himself with a stroll down the Strip. Wonderful late-afternoon light enveloped him, made him one of Haring's radiant babies. Whence this buoyancy that had him walking on the balls of his feet? New York dread, lifted?

No one else was on foot save for those who had just parked their cars or were returning to them, jingling keys to ward off pedestrian juju. In Los Angeles, Frank sensed, to walk for the sake of walking is to tear the social fabric.

Meanwhile, drivers slouched out of sight or popped up sociably, eyeing him curiously, except that at intersections they scowled as he crossed: To have to touch the brakes, when motion is *orgasmic?*

Seeing a new city gives you a fleeting fix on who you are. Frank came at L.A. fortified with the intensified sense of self nourished by New York City, where you need every morsel to withstand the daily assaults of a place where everything's a fight.

But in the curving golden washes and shadowy escapes of Sunset Boulevard, Frank felt his identity offer to levitate, to detach itself as though it were a construct and not intrinsic. Interesting, he thought; what could he metamorphose to? He looked at the soluble personalities within view: One of *them?*

At nightfall's first distant crackle of gunfire he was back at La Mirada. He watched TV until Conor came in. Conor dropped his briefcase, ordered their dinner from room service, took a shower, and ate wrapped in a towel on the end of the bed, watching newscasters baby-talk through the day's chases and drive-bys. He was tired, Frank's presence already taken for granted.

When they snuggled in bed Conor ignored his advances.

"What you got there?" he asked when Frank persisted. "Inflammation of the joint?"

"Spousal visitation, remember? We've been apart for –"

"Dolls –" Conor began with an edge to his voice. But he let it go in a sigh. "I know. Don't know what it is. It's this club thing. Playing it by ear."

"Sorry," Frank said. "Don't mean to complain."

They ate breakfast in the Space Age diner next door before Frank set off for a day's exploration. The sun was strong, but had a peculiar smog-muffled quality.

He boarded a bus that eventually meandered downtown. After wandering a sterile office district, he discovered L.A.'s Broadway. Money might have marched away up Bunker Hill, but on Broadway and Main and Spring stood the fine buildings of the ambitious young city, now turned over to bustling street-level emporia with signs painted colors of the rainbow.

And bordering them he found an enormous plain of Skid Row hotels—a Bowery blown up in size, its sidewalks etched with stench and filth like radiation burns. When he turned back downtown he saw a sign's rusty iron taunt against the sky: *The Million-Dollar Hotel.*

A long wait in the sun impressed him again with the contempt Los Angeles holds for those who use its public transit. It produced a sweltering bus into whose mass of standing humanity he had to wedge himself.

Back at the hotel Frank at first thought the maid had missed their room. The bedcover was kicked to the floor, the sheets roiled. Then he noticed Kleenex beside the pillows and a bottle of hand cream, and recognized a set piece familiar from New York. From beneath a sheet peeked a man in a magazine staring fiercely around as he spread his anus. In the VCR was a tape called *Pizza to Cum.*

Pressing *Play*, he watched a naked youth rub semen over another's back. Rewinding it some, and borrowing a dollop of Jergens, he brought himself off where Conor presumably had, as a young man ejaculated copiously in close up. He used the Kleenex, then channel-surfed until Conor returned and they ate dinner. There seemed no point in saying anything.

The next day began with drizzle that made the city look like wet paper.

Frank followed the Walk of Fame along Hollywood Boulevard, finding its brass-on-terrazzo stars treacherously slick. At the Chinese Theater he paid his respects to the fossilized footprints and handprints of movie stars, even more like gravestones than the Walk of Fame. Do they ever change them, he wondered? Choose some star's moment of eclipse to jackhammer her spoor to dust?

He caught the movie. When he came out the sun was slapping down shadows, skateboarders in low baggy pants like plus-fours working their way down the sidewalk sounding like railroad cars. "Fucking white man," one said as Frank passed.

He walked up Los Feliz Boulevard to Griffith Park, doused at intervals by sprinklers chugging across the sidewalk. When one spattered him while a householder stood by, waiting to open his Mercedes until Frank moved safely off, he remonstrated with him. "Not my problem," the man answered.

Dogs meanwhile hit the fences hard, barking percussively in clouds of spittle. The ring of dogs hitting fences is a sound as characteristic of Los Angeles as windchimes.

Griffith Park, Frank knew, is the biggest city park in America, but he was astonished to find it nothing like a larger Central Park, but a vast desert ridge. Tremendous!

He hiked steep paths up to the Observatory and to the top of Mount Hollywood. Canyons were carved into hills to every side, overlapping ridgelines painting gray against gray in oily mists. A green worm of smog writhed along the edges of the L.A. Basin. Overhead a police helicopter briefly hovered, a downdraft giving its rotors the sound of a machine gun. Near by, giant white boards spelled out *Hollywood.*

Frank descended to an old, disused road cut through lush groves of pine and eucalyptus. Three coyotes crossed in front of him. For several miles, as evening clarified the light and released exotic scents and the air acquired a champagne snap, he felt a peace that New York never vouchsafes.

Then he came across an area where men passed rigid as robots or stood against trees with mask-like expressions. Hearing a cough in the foliage, he turned to find a naked young man squeezing his erection at him. Frank stopped. He felt repelled, of course, but even more strongly felt — his roots being watered.

He wavered, but went home as night fell suddenly with tangible weight. Helicopters moved on searchlight stilts. At Hollywood and Vine, other searchlights creakily (and rather pathetically) emerged from an automated installation to swab the skies.

Their room was again a crime scene. Frank didn't disturb it.

Conor came home exhausted. He showered and they ordered dinner.

"You OK, Dolls?" Conor asked, but Frank wanted to wait until after they'd eaten. A waiter wheeled in their meal, with a beer for Frank and Conor's Coke (he drank alcohol only in bars). Over the TV they chatted about paint and carpeting and cash registers.

After pushing the trays into the hall, Frank said, "Conor, I was in Griffith Park today and saw a naked guy jerking off at me, and I wanted to — in fact, I *almost* — "

"Want to, Dolls? Go for it! Why the fuck tell *me* about it?"

"Because I'm faithful to you."

"Goody for you, but I repeat: Why tell *me* about it?"

"As your lover, my sex life's your business."

"No, it's not."

"Do you mean that?"

"Shit," said Conor. "Jesus *Christ.* Here we go!"

"Every day you leave our room so I'll come back and see you've been jerking off."

"Beats the park."

"But it hurts me. Clearly you mean it to. One reason I'm in this relationship is for sex. Which has been a laugh for a long time. If it's not going to give me any—I don't know what to do."

Conor appeared bored. His eyes flicking towards the TV, he punched the remote to louder it (his apt term) and spoke over its histrionics.

"Want dick, Dolls? *Go* for it. I forgive you, already."

He marched up the channels in the search that never ends.

"But we're faithful."

"I'm saying it's OK if you're *not*. Unless, as usual, I'm saying the wrong thing?" He loudered it some more. "Shit, Frank, not man enough for you? So sorry, but what can I do? What you do with your body, I don't care—it's *yours*."

"Could you lower it, please?"

"What?"

Frank found himself shouting, "Could you please LOWER THE VOLUME?"

Conor raised his eyebrows as he took the sound down to nothing.

"Come on, Conor, don't be weird."

"Oh, *you* want to jack off in the park, but *I'm* the weird one?"

"I want to have sex with *you*."

"Not tonight, Dolls, I'm bushed."

"I love you."

"Yeah, well, with love there's two sides to the story," Conor said, the volume swelling again.

"Why can't *our* love include a physical expression?"

The TV boomed.

"*Sex?*" Conor sneered.

Frank was astonished at the complexity of the expression clamping Conor's handsome face like hives. But it was momentary. Now there was a world of pain, then nothing, his eyes once again the shutters to his soul.

Frank grabbed the remote, hit *Off* and threw it across the room.

"Conor, if you'd just let me under your skin a little—"

"Nobody fucks *me*," Conor said. Rolling off the bed, he found the remote and plunged them back into Pandemonium. Worse, he found a hotel porn channel Frank had been innocent of until then. The camera probed between a woman's legs, Conor watching as though the answer were about to unfold.

"What's going on?" Frank shouted. "We're in Hollywood, so it has to be a bad movie?" The sound came down marginally. "You make it so hard to talk to you."

"I'm not articulate like you."

"That's a low blow."

"*Sorry.*"

The screen changed abruptly. Discontinuous noise filled the room at the flash of every new channel.

"I hate this place," Frank declared.

"I *like* it."

"L.A.'s a child's version of New York. Have you noticed how the guys here present themselves? At an angle, hair mussed, neck craned, features blurred? Too cute ever to be pinned down?"

"I *like* the guys here. Wish *you'd* get the fuck out. Go back to New York and out of my life. I've got work to do."

"Fine," Frank said.

He packed with care, disdaining to show haste. He should

have disdained to speak.

"You have to *care*, Conor," he said. "You have to *embrace* life."

"Whatever," Conor said, eyes glued to the TV. "It's all I can do to embrace *fate*."

Downstairs the clerk looked amused when Frank returned his key and asked him to call a cab. He rode to the airport sore that his relationship with Conor had ended, but accepting that it had, and even seeing how it was stillborn from the start. He had fallen for Conor out of his own need, which invented everything it required. Perhaps the same was true on Conor's part, too.

After a long night at LAX, as Los Angeles endured the mists and fogs that pass there for dawn, he found a seat on a New York–bound plane. The sun was rising as the jet corkscrewed out of that strange and tragic place so deceptively laced with elements of Paradise. Sunrise reddened the basin's edges as though hellfire were licking at them.

Meanwhile, Conor was left furious and worked up. Too worked up to sleep. Getting dressed, he cabbed to a bar in Silver Lake he knew about.

It was just what he wanted. *Home. Family.* Sitting at the bar drinking Scotch and brandy, he watched men mill about, carrying around the room glistening pectorals and tattoos the color of tropical flowers. He made friends with the bartender, whose face was highlighted in steel pins. Conor felt loose and fine, his burdens back in New York, or headed there.

He took to the dance floor, where the beat quickened and Madonna started to sing. Men flooded around him as, smiling, he moved to that insidious beat that promises to beat forever. He saw, or thought he saw, a staircase spiral down from the ceiling and Madonna herself descend it, and admired beneath her skirt the impressive hang of her cock and balls.

Men began to reach for him, to tug and unbutton and delve. They pulled off his shirt and he trod upon it, and in rhythm set about losing his jeans. Rising and rising, he danced and laughed, laughed and danced, down at last to the thing itself.

32.

JOEY WAS IN TROUBLE after the Crash. The IPO granted him options on 25,000 shares of Gag Reflex, Inc. at $4 apiece, but because SEC regulations forbade his exercising them for six months, Siggy Brewster had kindly advanced him secret ownership of 25,000 shares. The soaring stock price Joey counted on made the interest rate on Siggy's loan irrelevant.

So the morning after, he woke up to find that he owed Siggy more than $100,000 for stock that, sold that day, would buy an exquisite dinner for two.

His orthopedist, Dr. Pechter, shook his head with professional admiration at Joey's MRI.

"Amazing how one sneeze could do that," he marveled, before prescribing bed rest and a fancy new chair for the office.

Weeks on his back at home failed to do much to ease Joey's pain.

"I feel cut in two," he complained. "Cut in two and basted with red pepper."

When he returned to work, his new chair seemed only to aggravate his pain. It was of a style briefly popular, where one kneeled, resting one's bottom against a pad and holding the spine straight with old-fashioned muscle. Joey could find five minutes' surcease thus, but it was followed by hours of agony.

Every morning he did Dr. Pechter's exercises until he wept. Every night was torture. The only bearable parts of his day were his self-medicating hot soaks, a pitcher of margaritas beside the tub to cool him off.

He decided to undergo a disk fusion operation. Dr. Pechter objected that he was too young to resort to surgery.

"Maybe you could live with this pain," Joey told him, "but I can't. Wish I could, but I *can't.*"

Joey sucked on the anesthesia as the first happiness he'd known in a long time. He woke up hurting, but this was to be expected. Six days later he went home with a satisfied surgeon and high hopes.

Soon he was back at work, in worse pain than before. The change was scary. He had an air of having been shattered into fragments and clumsily put back together. His face a contorted, emaciated mask, he was incapable of concentrating—deeply distracted, always. He projected the same sense of something feeding on him as did the young men to be seen in ever increasing numbers around town sporting canes or wheelchairs and jaunty fedoras meant to hide their lesions. The sight of him gave Rex the willies.

One morning he returned for a post-op MRI. Afterwards Dr. Pechter was all smiles.

"Great news, Joey: Your spine now has fewer anomalies than the average *normal* one. T3, T4 and T5 fused *perfectly*. Nothing's bulging. I know you're reporting pain, but according to this—you shouldn't."

Joey nodded and left. It hurt too much to argue.

He hobbled towards the office; walking was fractionally less agonizing than being jounced around a bus or taxi. Up First Avenue he met a church bell tolling a funeral. The hearse driver, after impatiently checking his watch, fixed his gaze on him.

Joey found himself in Times Square studying movie marquees. *Dirty Dancing* was still playing at the Embassy 47th Street.

He called the office.

"Perri, I'm just out of the doctor's."

"What's he say?"

"Operation was a complete success."

"Oh Joey, I'm so *glad*."

"But I'm all in. Taking the day off."

"Just so you feel better."

Buying a ticket, Joey loaded up with popcorn and Pepsi, and went upstairs. The steeply raked seats poised him atop a ski jump, but the floor's sticky grip held him while the movie's noise knocked his troubles aside. Coming out afterwards to the disorienting sunshine, he stood apart from the sidewalk's current, considering what to do.

A beggar his age, wrapped in burlap, his ass hanging out, smells emanating, targeted him.

"C'mon, man, need 18 cents for the subway."

Joey often gave money to panhandlers, but today it was unbearable.

"Fuck you," he said, and walked away.

"What did you say? *Fuck* me?"

Apparently the beggar was also having a bad day. He kept pace with Joey, screaming into his face from a toothless red wound of a mouth. People stared. It was nightmarish.

Joey spoke conciliatingly.

"Look, I'm in a hurry —"

He felt in his pocket for change. There was none.

"Owe me apology, *motherfucker*."

Joey could smell his shit and see his ass and even the

sizable root of his organ. The beggar may have been no longer a man, but he wasn't living in pain, and therefore Joey envied him. It was unendurable. He bopped him one and ran like hell around the corner, hoping he didn't catch any germs.

He ate a late lunch at *Café Un Deux Trois*. Naturally he ran into friends and had fun holding forth on the prospects (not so brilliant, it seemed) of Gag Reflex, Inc. and telling some bitterly funny stories about Rex. The margaritas helped.

Cabbing home, he had to empty his wallet to the driver.

Phil was about to leave for his shift.

"Home already?"

"Back's killing me."

"What's the doctor say?"

"There's no hope."

"Bummer."

Joey went to bed with more margaritas and channel-surfed. Nothing on. He was napping when Phil returned after midnight with a huge anchovy and garlic.

"How you feeling, lover?"

"Ouch."

"Pizza?"

"Yeah."

They shared it in bed watching HBO, and eventually Joey found himself feeling full, blurred, fuzzy, warm. He wanted nothing ever to change.

As one movie ended and before the next began he strolled into the bathroom, energized by the fanfare worthy of the Last Judgment that was washing golden particles across the screen to coalesce into planets, constellations, galaxies, film reels, finally — apex of the known universe — HBO's logo. He opened his new bottle of Percodan, dumped pills into his palm and swallowed them as fast as he could.

"Hurry up," Phil yelled. "Movie!"

Pleased with himself, belching softly, Joey returned to bed. Phil hurriedly used the toilet. Noticing the empty bottle, he called, "Joey, what happened to your Percodan?"

"Bottle's empty, I'll get more tomorrow."

"Thought you *got* the refill."

"Starting!"

A few minutes later Joey said something under his breath.

"What?" Phil asked. They were lying spoonwise, curled as fetally towards the screen as Joey's spine would permit.

"Fuckers," he repeated distinctly.

He was skirting the edge of blackness. It had the companionable curve and texture of Richard Serra's sculpture *Tilted Arc,* which Joey came to know during jury duty when he ate his lunch in its shadow in Foley Square. The famous light radiated darkly farther along the curve as he hugged his way along it.

Waking up when Perri asked the answering machine where Joey was, Phil knew before he opened his eyes. He turned over and there was what used to be Joey, head back, cold even to sight, flesh livid where it met the sheets, the face drowned and unhappy.

"Fucker!" Phil said, hitting Joey's side hard. *"Fucker! fucker! fucker! fucker! fucker! fucker!"*

The funeral took place in the rural New Jersey town where Joey grew up, at a church in gently rolling countryside lovely even in mid-winter. It was an austere barn of a place outside, but had a warm wooden interior.

Frank arrived via bus from the Port Authority, having worked out the intricate schedule in a new access of patience. Phil, standing on the steps, introduced him to Joey's stricken siblings and white-haired mother, who repeated to him as to everyone else, "We don't know *what* happened. We may *never* know."

Several distinct groups made up the crowd. Most were local folk: playmates, classmates, friends of the family. But there were New York contingents, too, of record-company people, Gag Reflex staff, comedians, musicians, drag queens not known to have seen daylight (or set foot in Jersey) for years. Frank saw Rosetta Stone stepping out of a Daimler parked next to Rex's superstretch.

He took a pew behind Rex, who was flanked by Ashley and a very slender Perri. Tapping him on the shoulder, he and Rex exchanged sad greetings. Rex looked great: confident, assured, beautifully groomed; the very triangles under his eyes gleamed. And yet from somewhere Frank caught a whiff of strain, as though a price is to be paid for the life of untrammeled id, of hungers unappeasable.

Perri, he thought, resembled Bianca Jagger, sexy and strong. At one point Ashley turned around to look past him with a face queerly blanked out. When her left eye changed direction the right eye popped and revolved before trawling lazily after it, like a Looney Tunes character's trademark tic. She kept a hand on Rex's arm.

Belatedly, Frank realized that the man in a ponytail next to Perri was Conor. He reached to touch him. Conor nodded.

Rosetta found Frank's ear from behind.

"What a waste to *bury* Joey," she whispered. "Roast him in his own juices, succulent like you wouldn't believe. *Gnnnh . . . Gnnnh . . .*"

He blinked so as to register her wit.

"Heard you and Conor broke up."

"Yes."

"Whose idea was it?"

"Mutual."

"Uh-huh. They say the L.A. club's losing money?"

"Oh, really? Give it time."

The service seemed to Frank (though no aficionado) a stripped-down requiem Mass, perhaps the result of negotiating for a patch of sacred ground. There was a boys choir, and Racquel stepped forward to sing *The End of Time* ("For my funeral," Joey had said, and Rex didn't forget).

But what really wrung the tears was the choir's following Joey's other longstanding, if joking, wish. Over an organ obbligato, the boys joined hands and sang:

> $M-I-C$...

"*C*? See you real soon," came a soprano warble.

> $K-E-Y$...

"*Y*? Because we *like* you."

> $M-O-U-S-E$.
> *Mickey Mouse,*
> *Mickey Mouse.*

"Disney would have a fucking shitfit," Rex murmured happily.

Frank caught a ride to the cemetery with friends of Joey's rich in lore of high school's weed and tequila. There they watched his casket slide off the hearse to become a weight borne over buckled ground by his brothers, Rex, Phil and Conor. The hole that awaited it was outrageously raw, except where Astroturf disguised its edges. As the casket sank into blackness snow began to fall. White particles detached themselves from the sky and sprinkled the dirt.

Frank had no heart to join the family for a meal, so waited for the bus, watching snow fall more and more rapidly.

Finally he was back in the city, where there was no need to think about how Joey's first night underground was under a blanket of snow as well. In the city there was no snow.

33.

HARSHAW'S BILL, delayed beyond Rex's wildest hopes by machinery he had no conception of, arrived at last one day in February.

Harshaw dispatched it with his firm's elderly messenger. Jacob shambled into the office after lunch to laughter on all sides. He was eager to dispense a tip on Hialeah, but going from hand to hand feeding the hilarity was the *Post*'s front page.

MAN-EATER BITES

read the headline, over a photograph of a startled Rosetta Stone in shackles beside a car's open trunk. The story explained how undercover ATF agents stung her: She was buying untaxed bottles of liquor out of a car with North Carolina plates when they swooped down with assault rifles to make the arrest.

Another picture showed The Last Laugh's front doors chained shut.

"And whose name's on the liquor license?" Rex was asking. "*Siggy's?* Guess again: Bitch is going to *prison.*"

Jacob kept his horse to himself, but handed Byrne an envelope crammed with Harshaw & Crowfoot's bill, payable upon receipt, and sat down to await the check.

Byrne held the envelope out to Trish, and Trish waved it at Rex, who plucked it from her hand. He grimaced—he knew what it was—but it's the lot of the mogul to get the big bills.

"Drumroll, please," he requested.

Byrne obliging, Rex opened the envelope, leafed past the cover letter to the bill's summary page, and went pale, staggered (but not surprised) at the figure there: $368,541.07. He gurgled.

"Black!" said Perri.

"Give me the telefuckingphone," he managed.

Jacob brought out a *Racing Form*.

Byrne had returned to his call, but Rex grabbed the phone out of his hands, mashed the keypad and clamped it to his head, his eyes bulging; Byrne said nothing. Naturally what Rex heard was, "Barbra will *never* age, she refuses to!"

Throwing the receiver into its cradle with a roundhouse right, he dialed again. "The number you have dialed—" began a prissy voice.

He picked up the entire PBX unit, and only Byrne's death grip on it prevented him from smashing it to the floor.

"Get Harshaw," Rex told Trish through clenched teeth as he returned to his office. "What balls. *I* should've gone to fucking law school."

Trish dialed and a few moments later nodded through the open glass doors. Perri watched closely as Rex picked up, his face a rictus.

Crossing his legs, Jacob went to work on Santa Anita.

"Hey, Harshaw, your little invoice arrived."

"Yes?"

"That all you *got?*"

"If you're disputing—"

"Not disputing a fucking thing! I saw the hours you put in, skinning the regs here, skirting the law there."

Rex always paced during serious calls, going at the wall, then veering away, the better to force energy over the wire. His eyes saw nothing as he threw himself into his voice.

"Hey, *granted,* tedious work," he went on, *"million* details to chase down and dress up, but it wasn't building the Brooklyn *Bridge,* it was writing a *prospectus,* that's what you fucking *do.*

"Meanwhile on the Street I'm roadkill. Last I saw—and you *do* realize I'm talking *pink* sheets, NASDAQ fucking *delisted* us?—*3/64ths* asked, *1/64th* bid. Can you tell me what that comes to in American money?"

"You do the math, Rex. Not my problem. *Had* your shot. Think I like working for a deadbeat? If you're not sending a check back, tell Jacob to come on in, won't you?"

"Hold on, I got it: Times shares outstanding, means my company is worth, give or take, a brand-new Plymouth *Reliant.*"

"Look, we worked, good faith, on something that unfortunately you failed to pull off. Let me patch Siggy in."

"What do we need *that* cocksucker for?"

"Hi, Rex," said Siggy dryly.

"Let me point out something so simple even you assholes ought to be able to get it," Rex said. *"My company's worth less than your fucking bill!* For legal expertise creating a company worth *shit,* you have the fucking *balls* to bill me $368,541.07? Though I admit—the seven cents? *Genius.*"

"Seven cents is seven cents, Rex," Siggy put in. "Might remember that, next time."

"You're fucking a corpse, Siggy! That what you like? Nice chilly body, doesn't pass remarks on your limp little Wall

Street dick? Never liked you either, Harshaw: Your farts are the smelliest, should see a doctor. *I can't pay this bill and stay in business.*"

"Rex, here's what's going down," said Siggy. "We're taking Gag Reflex, Inc. private."

"*Private?* Just took it fucking *public!* I'm your fucking *client*, remember?"

"Carried out our agreement to the letter, and now The Cromwell Companies have been retained to acquire it as a privately-held entity."

"Retained by *who?*" Rex asked. "Who's doing this to me, Siggy? Who's cutting off my dick and stuffing it down my throat?"

"Shit, Siggy, Jacob fucked up," said Harshaw. "Rex, ask Jacob for the other envelope."

Bewildered, Rex did as he was told, and with apologies Jacob found an envelope in his bag that he handed over, saying, "This one I need signed for."

Rex tore it open to find a summons and complaint, both incomprehensibly captioned *Black v. Black*. He gaped.

"Rex? Still there, Rex?" Siggy was asking. "Wife's a smart lady. Not my fault, betrayal is the *law*: Darwin."

It dawned on Rex that he'd been served with divorce papers. As Perri had thrown him out of their apartment weeks earlier and had his belongings hauled to Ashley's (and him billed for it), his surprise was touching.

But concentrated into that moment was terrible pain. The result was unexpected: Rex began to shed his clothing. He tore off his tie and whipped it at the bullpen. Ripping his shirt off in a fusillade of buttons, he balled it up and threw it after the tie.

"Trying to *fuck* me?" he yelled into the phone. "You can't fuck *me!* It cannot be done! CANNOT BE DONE!"

The wire snapped at the last word. He hurled the receiver at a gold record and glass shattered. Trish and Byrne retreated to the conference room.

"That *goddam* flatulent motherfucker pettifucking *schmuck* son of a slimy-cunted whore *LAWYER!*" Rex bellowed. He threw his undershirt at the wall. "As for *Siggy—*"

"Black," said Perri from the threshold.

He paid her no heed. Taking a breath he heaved at his table. Creaking with the outrage of a sinking ship, it crashed onto its side, pottery shattering and papers flying into the air before finding new equipoise on the floor.

Only then did he turn towards Perri, squaring himself like a kung fu master.

"*You!*"

"Calm down, Black."

"I *am* calm!" he shouted, hurling a shoe at her. It missed.

She ran around the table. His other shoe went flying through a window in a shower of glass. He chased her, but couldn't catch her. They circled the table until he stopped in rage and frustration.

"This what you want, Perri? My *all* isn't *enough* for you?"

He tugged at his belt and smacked it at her, with exaggerated grunts pulled off his pants and resumed the chase holding them high, waving in the wind, until he stuffed them through the broken pane. He tore off his socks, tossed them aside, stepped out of his shorts and pushed them, too, into 57th Street.

"Stop it, Black!"

"Just giving you what you *want*, Perri, which is everything I ever fucking *had*."

"Still need that signed for," Jacob remarked to no one.

Rubbing his belly and cleaning his navel, apparently unaware that he was nude, Rex regarded his wrecked office.

Suddenly he darted into the closet and tore his jacket off its hanger, came back, pushed it out the window and leapt up on the sill to follow its flight.

Bracing himself, he watched with glee as the air teased it, briefly lifted it, filled its sleeves and sent them flailing in Armani splendor to the pavement. A bus ran over it, and Rex, buttocks flexing, rattled the panes in triumph.

Across the street in Carnegie Hall a dance class happily crowded the windows, watching him.

Speaking in a tone meant to calm a crazed animal, Perri reached up for his hand and pressed fingers to the small of his back, while telling him there was no other way for the company to survive, that her takeover was best for them both and especially for their child, that in Chapter 11 she could shed management contracts and out-of-town leases, get a break on back rent, keep the New York club going on a solidly profitable basis.

Rex couldn't follow the sense of what she said, but the melody of her voice assuaged and soothed his despair. He allowed her to pull at his hand and, suddenly ashamed, cupping his genitals, he stepped clumsily to the floor and settled on the rug. Tears pumped from his eyes as he buried his face in his elbow.

"For want of a fucking *nail*," he wailed. "The whole fucking house that *Jack* built! Fuck, fuck, *fuck*, I've been *fucked*. Oh God, I'm sorry, I'm so *sorry*."

Perri worked Clarissa (shrieking with glee as she watched her dad) into coat and hat and scarf and placed her in her stroller. Then she found that grimy raincoat belonging to nobody that hangs in every New York office closet. Stooping beside Rex, murmuring as to an infant, she threaded his arms through the sleeves and stood him up, buttoned the buttons, folded the lapels and closed the belt with a twist.

Pushing Clarissa ahead of her, pausing only to sign Jacob's receipt, she led him out.

They got on the elevator. Rex's arms hung limp at his sides and his eyes were dull. Others got on at a lower floor but appeared to notice nothing amiss. At the street door Reuben, the doorman, eyeing his bare feet and shins, tossed hair and streaked face, asked, "Everything OK, Mr. Black?"

Puzzled by the question, but instantly energized, Rex looked Reuben in the eye and smiled. He won a smile in return. His courage may have deserted him for ten minutes, but it was back. Appetite was sure to follow.

"Everything's super, Reuben. Just *super*."

www.ingramcontent.com/pod-product-compliance
Lightning Source LLC
Chambersburg PA
CBHW061616100726
47898CB00002B/684